VENETIAN TRILOGY

Jeremy Gent

La Fuga

The Escape

Jeremy Gent

authorHOUSE®

AuthorHouse™ UK Ltd.
500 Avebury Boulevard
Central Milton Keynes, MK9 2BE
www.authorhouse.co.uk
Phone: 08001974150

First published by AuthorHouse 11/14/2011

ISBN: 978-1-4567-8424-9 (sc)

PART THREE
LA FUGA

(THE ESCAPE)

Introduction

This is the story of Gianna Ambrosio, daughter of Marco and Isabella, who was born in Venice in the middle of 1945 just after the end of Second World War in Europe. It is based around the private diaries she kept and the recollections of her younger sister, Luisa. It was only a few months after Gianna started living in London that she started keeping a diary, which ran from the beginning 1965 up until her death in early August 1968, when she was only twenty-three years old. These diaries only came into Luisa's possession when she was given them by John Smith, their half brother.

They were written in German, a language that Gianna spoke fluently and which her husband Carlo did not speak at all. Luisa also spoke German as fluently as her sister did. The reason for sticking to her second language in the writing of these diaries will become apparent. They were amongst John's mother Hayley's possessions, and he thought that they should be returned to Gianna's family. It was fortunate that during her life, Hayley didn't learn to speak German either, as she also features prominently inside them (albeit under a code name, which wasn't difficult to recognise). The reason for this is that these diaries do not flatter Hayley at all. Luisa obtained most of the information regarding the early years of the story from her own family and friends and wartime colleagues of her father and their children, as well as her own memories from childhood. She is the main storyteller.

CHAPTER 1

Marco

My father, Marco Ambrosio, was born in March 1921 but never knew his own father, who left his wife, my grandmother, a few months after he was born. It is not surprising, therefore, that grandmother never liked to talk about the past, and as a result it was difficult to find out very much about my grandfather and their life together. But from what I was able to gather from her, Grandfather, like millions of others who lived through the conflict, suffered badly in the fighting in the First World War. He listened to the rallying cries of the demagogues of the era, like D'Annunzio and Mussolini, and joined up like a true patriot in May 1915, as soon as war was declared against Austria-Hungary. He survived, despite the terrible conditions and the various battles of the River Isonzo valley (I am told there were twelve in total but don't think he could have been in every single one), where he saw much suffering in what turned out to be a pointless and costly conflict in terms of lives sacrificed for a gain that many did not live to see. He also fought in the South Tyrol and in the Dolomites, where the conditions were also atrocious, made worse by the freezing cold climate high up in the mountains.

Grandfather was, like all of my family, Venetian and possibly had a greater degree of understanding than many of the main war aims because the conflict was fought much nearer to where he lived. When he was young, he was brought up to dislike anything to do with the Austrians, who had originally been responsible for ending the Venetian Republic, and also to distrust the French, who had occupied large areas of Italy in the past and used Venice as a bargaining chip, having threatened more than once to destroy it. The Habsburgs had occupied and governed the Serenissima, as Venice is often referred to, as recently as 1866, when after yet another war, it was first ceded to France and then handed over to Italy after a plebiscite of dubious validity.

Most of those who went to fight had little idea of even where they were located. I wonder how a Sicilian peasant, used to the warm Mediterrancan climate of his island, would have possibly coped; many, of course, did not. Whatever Grandfather's level of political understanding or knowledge of geography, he must however have become very disillusioned at the way the ordinary Italian peasant soldier was treated. To this day, many Italians will give the impression, especially to foreigners, that they do not have much of an appreciation of what the fighting with Austria-Hungary was all about, only that it cost a lot of lives. I don't know if this is because they are sad or are ashamed of what happened, or just want to forget all about it; probably all three. There is no real desire amongst us ordinary Italians to talk about it.

As in the United Kingdom, France, and Belgium, there are war memorials in every Italian city, town, and village. This is so in every other country that was caught up in the war that was supposed to end all wars. I often wonder how many more generations these monuments to the folly of the past will last; some say forever, but there will surely come a day, many years from now, when the current generation no longer connects in such a strong way with what happened. Perhaps say in another hundred years' time, it will no longer have the same impact. I do not mean to be disrespectful, but generations do eventually pass on, and the rights and wrongs of the past fade into insignificance.

But try to imagine the Italian soldiers of 1915. They were mainly made up of illiterate peasants placed into an army with only the bare fundamentals of training. They were told that the war was necessary to unite the areas that had a large Italian-speaking population, those of Trento and Trieste. There were tales (some true, others invented) of persecution of ethnic Italians, many of whom it was said were living in misery in these areas, without the protection of the Italian flag. Italy was still only a young country, having formed in 1871 during an epoch that was known as the *Risorgimento*, which basically means revival: a reference to the re-emergence of the Italian-speaking people. As you can imagine, the main component of this revival was nationalism, which became the driving force as Italians united under one banner.

But the war aims of the politicians in terms of territorial ambitions went deeper than just capturing Italian-speaking areas, because Italy wanted to be the main power in the Adriatic. The Treaty of London, which basically brought my country into the war on the side of the Allies, promised also Istria, most of the Dalmatian coast, and a foothold in Albania to Italy on conclusion of the conflict.

In some of these new areas of territorial ambition, there were only isolated pockets of Italians, which could not even be described to be living in communities. In fact, they were more like infiltrators.

Previously, my country had been allied with, or at least had an understanding with, the Central Axis powers of Germany and Austria-Hungary in what was known as the Triple Alliance, but relationships had always been uneasy with the Habsburg Austrians over just where the northern borders with Austria should lie. In the view of many historians, we changed sides to get a better deal—an understandable analysis of the situation, but the politics were more complicated than just that.

The war became a stalemate, and it seemed that by the time the failed summer offensives in 1917 had ground to a halt, the war could not be won by the Allies. It felt like the war might go on for many more years. The Russian Empire withdrew from the conflict following the revolution and overthrow of the tsar and tsarina, releasing the German divisions tied up on that front for diversion to west in France and to the south in Italy. This extra million or so soldiers was going to give the German army the edge that it needed to win the war, but luckily for the Allies, the United States joined the fighting on the Western Front in 1917, and this tipped the balance back in their favour.

When this happened, the Americans took over large parts of the line previously held by the French army, which was by now close to exhaustion and not able to go on the offensive after having mutinied earlier in the year following yet another failed offensive on the Chemin des Dames. The British were also thankful for the arrival of the Americans, as their army was exhausted following a costly action at Arras, in support of the failed French offensive, and then the battle that nearly broke the spirit of the fighting soldiers in the mud of Flanders. The Germans were still able to mount their offensive in 1918 ("*Grosse Schlact in Frankreich*"), but after an initial breakthrough, it petered out and failed to win the war.

The tide turned against the German army in the summer of 1918, and it fell back in retreat under weight of the determination of the Allies with huge materiel assistance from the Americans. But the appearance of the Americans came with various strings attached. They had a totally different view of the way that Europe would look after the successful conclusion of the war, and it was at odds with the original promises laid down in the Treaty of London that ensured that Italy would abandon the Triple Alliance and come in on the side of the Allies. The problem for Italy was that its territorial ambitions went very much against the ideals of American President Woodrow Wilson, whose fourteen points for settling the Great War included self-determination and country boundaries that observed that important principle. This meant that they were not prepared to tolerate unjustified Italian expansion and *that* nation becoming the new power in the Balkans instead of the Austrian Habsburgs.

That said, after the Treaty of Versailles in 1919, my country ended up not only with Trento and Trieste but also with the Alto Adige, which the Austrians, the former occupiers, still to this day call Sud Tirol (South Tyrol). This particular concession went against what Wilson wanted but it compensated my homeland for the sacrifice it had made during the war, and it supposedly guaranteed its borders up to where the modern-day Brenner Pass connects the two countries. The other territorial wishes and demands were not granted at Versailles, much to the bitter regret of Italian President Orlando, who was overcome with grief because in his own mind he had failed his country. In the new deal, it was no good thinking that the promises of the Treaty of London would be honoured in full. Now there would be no Italian presence in the Balkans, most of which became united under the newly created state of Jugoslavia.

When this became apparent, Orlando had difficulty in fully taking part in all the negotiations as the world map was carved up; all that mattered to him was Italy. He cared not for the sense of injustice felt by the majority in the Sud Tirol, where the main language is still German even today and the majority of the people are most definitely of Austrian or German descent (and proud to be so). After all, Orlando (and a few million others, it has to be said) reasoned that this was the price you must pay for defeat. At the time of the conflict, 89 percent of the population was German speaking and only 3 percent Italian—so much for self-determination when the land was ceded to Italy.

Although over the decades there has been an Italianisation of the region, the present government is careful to leave them alone in what is practically a self-governing province under the Italian flag. The banner of the province is still coloured red and white—the colours of the Tyrol. If on occasions you see an individual dressed somewhat incongruously in blue overalls then this is his way of stressing that he is a Tyrolean living under the occupation of the Italian state. When you visit some of the towns and villages, it feels like Austria, not Italy. It was not until 1992 that the question was finally resolved (helped by the fact that Austrian membership in the European Union later on in 1995 made the question of borders mostly irrelevant). Before then, the majority population had suffered varying degrees of persecution and ill-treatment, and this gave rise to a homegrown resistance movement that committed acts of terrorism to demonstrate protest and dissent. Today, all is peaceful but it takes many generations for feelings of resentment to subside, and if you can speak any German, it is far better to use it when you are in this area because it will ensure a better reception with the local people.

In the awful war on this front, my grandfather narrowly escaped execution for alleged cowardice during the retreat of the Italian army from the rout of Caporetto. This was later catalogued as the twelfth and final battle of the Isonzo and took place in October 1917. I cannot be sure of all the details in his individual case, but I am sure from the accounts that he was lucky to survive. Apparently, there was a policy of decimation within the Italian military. That is the shooting of front line soldiers when the high command perceived that there had been a lack of effort shown by the troops in battle. I thought that this was something that died out with the Roman legions but somehow, incredibly, it had survived into the first part of the twentieth century.

As a member of a defeated and retreating army, grandfather was singled out by a group of *Carabinieri* officers because he had lost his rifle. He explained desperately that he had lost his weapon when a shell exploded amongst a group of soldiers, and his first reaction was to try and save a comrade who needed evacuation.

The same shell had also sent small pieces of shrapnel flying into his arm, which was oozing blood in several places from wounds that had not been properly treated. He was able to show them this by rolling up the already tattered sleeve of his army uniform. He pleaded with the officers that he had a wife and (at that stage, before my father was born) two young children.

The officers listened and believed him, partly because the junior officer commanding his section came to his assistance and backed up his story. This often did not make any difference, but the officer had been a forceful character. And so it followed, Grandfather was fortunate and they took pity on him but shot his friend, a fellow soldier, instead. He was still carrying his rifle, and I suppose the reasoning was that a soldier who still had a gun to fire hadn't tried hard enough and had retreated instead of staying at his post to engage the enemy. The junior officer was also lucky to escape summary justice, as men of this rank were held responsible for the failure. The long bloody gash on his forehead, caused by flying shrapnel, was the probable reason for his life also being spared.

Grandfather saw many of these executions and the distressing sight of good soldiers, who had done nothing wrong, begging for their lives as he had done, usually to no effect as they were led away to be shot, crying as they went. The soldiers were brutalised and could also be executed for as little as complaining about the food, which was undeniably poor, or having their leave cancelled, which happened regularly. Some soldiers served throughout the conflict, three and a half years, without ever going home on leave. Unbelievable though it may seem, decimation was carried out in the name of retaining discipline. Sometimes, the selection of those soldiers to be murdered in this fashion was totally at random, meaning that brave, resourceful soldiers who had fought with courage and determination were executed along with the shirkers and cowards. This complete absence of justice had the impact of collapsing the morale and lessening the fighting spirit even more, the exact opposite of the desired outcome.

At Caporetto, which these days is in Slovenia, the military command of the Italian army was guilty of complacency and bungling on a grand scale. Even though an Austrian offensive was anticipated all along the Isonzo front, wrong decisions were consistently made by the High Command and lower down at the level of company commander. In the area where my grandfather was dug in, sheltering in an inadequate and filthy trench, the enemy was sighted in the distance, and in reality their troops were being moved up into position to launch an attack. However, it was assumed that they were just a column of prisoners being marched back behind the Italian front line. Communications were a constant problem during the Great War on every front, but in this case, nobody was ordered to check out what was going on.

In the offensive that followed, the Austrians were bolstered by experienced German divisions released from the Eastern Front with Russia. This was just what the Austrian army needed. At the start of the conflict, one famous German said that being allied to Austria-Hungary was like being shackled to a corpse.

Included in the ranks of the German army was a young lieutenant named Erwin Rommel, who featured strongly in the western desert and in Normandy in the next conflict some twenty-five years or so later. Using new storm trooper tactics, which had already been tried out first on the Western Front, the enemy broke through quite easily, and the resistance of a half-starved and inadequately led Italian army crumbled.

The energy, enterprise, and tactics of the German Wurttemburg Mountain Battalion in particular, of which Rommel was a member, enabled huge gains to be made, meaning all the Italian army could do was fall back in confusion, with large numbers surrendering without a fight. The Germans fought for almost two days without rest, and the territorial gains were immense. The Italian army had been geared to offensive operations and had difficulty in mounting defensive operations against the new tactics being used. The High Command put the blame on the front line soldiers for the disaster at Caporetto, although there were deficiencies throughout the structure of the Italian army that contributed to the severest setback in the whole of the campaign on this front during the conflict.

The terrible practice of decimation, therefore, continued during this disastrous retreat. Fortunately, the blaming of the troops for the failure of military tactics and demanding total, unquestioning obedience ended after Caporetto, when the general responsible, Luigi Cadorna, was relieved of his command and replaced by General Armando Diaz. Cadorna's lack of competence as a man fit for command had at last been exposed.

When I was in Milano with my second husband (who is English), we emerged from Milano Nord Station after an hour-long journey from Lake Como, where we had been on holiday, into the modern-looking Piazza Cadorna; he commented, "Fancy your government naming a square after that incompetent bastard. Is the main road leading off called 'Via Della Decimation'?"

I reminded him that he had shown me the statue of Field Marshall Earl Haig when he took me to London and walked me down Whitehall from Trafalgar Square.

"You said that all the old soldiers marching down to the Cenotaph on Armistice Day wouldn't have been too thrilled to see a statue of the man whose military tactics caused the death of so many of their friends and family."

"That's true," he acknowledged and added, "worldwide, we seem to honour people whether they deserve it or not. But I guess that's the establishment for you."

And indeed, Cadorna had been looked upon as a military genius by an unquestioning sycophantic High Command and by those politicians who simply didn't know any better. However, his removal immediately helped to improve morale in an army that was considered beaten and close to surrendering. The main cause of the idiotic conduct of the war was now removed. And as it turned out, the troops rallied, held the line on the River Piave north of Venice, and eventually went on to victory, bolstered in a small way by reserves of British and French divisions diverted from the Western Front.

But for my grandfather, the damage was done, and according to Grandmother, the death of many of his friends and the suffering he witnessed everywhere stayed with him for all the time he remained in the army and even more so afterwards. He had continued to serve the cause, taking part in the last major offensive of the war, the encounter at Vittorio Veneto, which ended in a resounding victory. The Austrians surrendered after this battle, after their government at home collapsed.

When Grandfather returned from the war, he tried to resume family life, but one day he just left without a trace and with no explanation. He used to have terrible nightmares, particularly reliving the hand-to-hand fighting that took place. I put it down to the fact that it was probably a complete mental breakdown, something that in those days would not have been understood in any shape or form. There were no support mechanisms in Italy for traumatised soldiers after the Great War. On the streets, a man with mental problems was to be avoided, not helped. Post-traumatic stress syndrome was not known about in those days. Indeed, it was only after the war that combat trauma was properly recognised under the term of "war neuroses," rather than the rather misleading term of "shell shocked." There was even a reluctance to accept the recognised diagnosis of neurasthenia during the conflict, because it was felt that if used as an excuse, it would weaken the fighting spirit.

I can only imagine the sense of injustice must have been huge for all soldiers on all sides. There could only have been feelings of betrayal that you had suffered appalling hardship and your country was not grateful. I can only draw the parallel of British soldiers returning to the land fit for heroes promised by Prime Minister David Lloyd George. This was a promise that was never kept.

Marco, my father, was only six months old when grandfather left and grew up a poor and unruly child, the youngest of three, largely without supervision from his mother, who had to take on a number of jobs just to provide for her young children. Grandmother tried to share the responsibility for looking after Marco with his brother and sister but they were too young to really know what to do. Grandfather later turned up as a corpse in the less-than-salubrious Pre District of Genoa. He had been murdered, and Grandmother had to identify his body, which she was barely able to do, as it had been so badly mutilated. Later she admitted to not being sure it was a correct identification but at the time, it allowed some badly needed financial benefits to be paid over to her.

Marco became even more rebellious when his mother took up with another man and remarried. Her new husband was a totally inoffensive man who tried to show warmth to all of the children, but this made no impression upon Marco, who wanted nothing to do with him. When approached, he was surly, rude, and disrespectful, and he showed wilful disobedience toward his mother. By way of retaliation against his mother's new way of life, Marco did much as he pleased and seldom bothered to go to school. The legacy of this was his inability to read or write very well, but according to everyone who knew him well, he was a good talker and, whenever necessary, a creative liar.

During the darkest period in the history of Italy, between the wars, Marco attached himself to the angry gangs of hooligans that had sworn allegiance to Il Duce, Benito Mussolini. When war came, he joined up and fought in Greece and North Africa. By the time Mussolini was deposed in 1943 and Italy joined the Allies, Marco had already changed sides and assisted the partisans in Sicily during the Allied invasion. I do not know what made him do this, but I rather suspect that he fell under the influence of some more sensible fellow soldiers or an educated officer, perhaps, who had guessed which way things were going. Ever the opportunist, Father would have jumped upon the nearest bandwagon. Although exposed to great danger, Marco looked upon this period as one of the happiest of his life. It was partly the comradeship but also the opportunity to have sex with as many Sicilian girls as possible, which he duly did. Many of these girls were starving and exchanged sex for food in order to stay alive. Food is power. This suited Marco very well indeed, despite the fact that he had already married Isabella in 1940.

He secretly returned to Venice in the autumn of 1944, sometime before the liberation, when the city was still under occupation. This was much to the surprise of Isabella, who thought that he was dead because she had neither heard from him nor received any money from him in over twelve months. He found out that Isabella had taken up with a member of the resistance in Venice and had been having a regular liaison with this man; the relationship had been going on for some time. He flew into a rage, and when he finally extracted a confession that she had also been having sex with him, he beat Isabella up, after which he raped her. The next day, he disappeared again and returned to join his unit. The direct result of this encounter was that Isabella became pregnant and gave birth to Gianna. It was a premature birth, and for a long time, Marco was convinced that Gianna was not his child. His injured pride was what made him believe that was the case.

Isabella stayed with Marco after the war because she felt there was no choice. She had guilty feelings about having betrayed Marco, despite the fact that she knew of his infidelities. He explained by way of self-justification that you never knew what the next day would bring when you were fighting the Germans, and you took your happiness whenever you could find it. Isabella no doubt said the same thing. He repeatedly reminded her that he had risked his life when he had come back to see her and that if he had been stopped and found to be with incorrect papers, he would have been shot.

He never mentioned the frequent gang rapes of Sicilian girls (some as young as twelve or thirteen) that he participated in with his partisan comrades. This activity continued during the liberation of Rome in June and Florence in August and a few times in between as well. I only found out about this after his death, from the sons of old soldiers who had served with him. At the time, these rapes were conveniently blamed on the Germans or the liberating Allied troops. I sought independent confirmation of these atrocities and only had this information about my father confirmed by his elder sister, who is in her eighties but still living in Padua, where she moved in 1948 after the war. She knew about these stories as well and was ashamed to say that Marco had boasted about his sexual prowess and the things he and his comrades got up to when they were down in the south and advancing up mainland Italy.

The other stories he used to tell her seemed to exaggerate his bravery in the face of the most appalling odds. I learned that in reality there were random killings of enemy soldiers who were surrendering or who were already prisoners. She had a very low opinion of her brother after those revelations and the bragging about how many enemy he had killed in combat. This was probably the reason we saw so little of her as we were growing up. She just couldn't stand him.

However, when the war ended, Marco became a successful travelling salesman, and this gave him plenty of opportunity to have affairs and consort with prostitutes, which he frequently did. When at home, he behaved like a spoilt child and treated Isabella with very little respect. Sexual encounters with her were fuelled by drink, and they were short, brutish affairs that she must have endured without any enjoyment. He became very angry when, some four years or so after the birth of Gianna, Isabella became pregnant again. I was born in 1950. The birth was very traumatic, and Isabella very nearly died. Apparently, my aunty living in Padua came back to Venice to nurse me and look after Gianna until Mamma was well again. Marco would not allow his own mother to assist because of the childish resentment he still harboured for her second husband.

The operation to save Isabella's life ensured that there would be no more pregnancies, which was a relief to them both, for very different reasons. Isabella found sexual relations with Marco even more difficult after she was fully recovered, and it angered him when he was unable to satisfy his lust. I can still remember the shouting and angry voices that leaked through the walls of their bedroom. This meant that he was always keen to get away and back to work where, on the road, he could live his other life.

On reflection, I bet that Mamma Isabella wished that she had the courage to leave Marco and take her chances with her resistance man. She may have thought this, but

I can vouch for the fact that she never actually said it (well, not to me). But sometimes you could read her face, especially after a bad row took place.

CHAPTER 2

ISABELLA

My mother, Isabella Belcapo, was born in the first hours of 1924. She was abandoned at birth by her mother, who was a prostitute, found and taken in, and brought up in an orphanage. Her mother never made any attempt to see her again. She was a very pretty child and grew into an attractive teenager. She was so good-looking that she attracted the wrong kind of attention at the home where she was raised. Isabella was subjected to sexual abuse but fortunately escaped the attentions of the main instigator, who was reported, arrested, and imprisoned before she became a servant to his sexual desires.

She left the orphanage at the age of thirteen when a well-to-do, upper-class Venetian family in the San Marco district offered her employment as a house girl. The family was kind, and she thrived in this new environment. They lived in a large old palazzo by the side of the Grand Canal, and Isabella was allocated a room of her own. She revelled in the freedom that this brought to her. It seemed that the children of the family loved Isabella more than their own mother and always wanted to be in her company. She was like an elder sister to them, and they insisted that she accompany them on family holidays. She was placed in a position of complete trust and never let her employer down, working very long hours to repay the trust that they put in her. These vacations were the only times that she spent outside of Venice and the lagoon. She was able to enjoy the delights of Tuscany and, one year, the nicer parts of the Bay of Naples when they stayed at Ravello.

At the age of sixteen, after the commencement of the war, she met a seemingly brave and handsome young soldier by the name of Marco Ambrosio, and before he went off to fight for his country, they secretly got married. As you know, a great number of people behave in this way when a country goes to war. Other than some of the disgusting characters she had encountered at the orphanage, this was the first man who paid her any real attention, and she instantly fell in love with him. She was underwhelmed by her initial experience of the marriage bed; these encounters were short, not to mention painful, and brought her no joy at all.

Marco returned home from two campaigns, and it was quite clear that the life of a soldier seemed to suit him despite the fact that the army appeared to be in retreat and the war was not going very well. He was certainly tough and prided himself always on being a survivor. I put it down to luck and his personal policy of never volunteering for anything dangerous.

While he was away, Isabella got caught up in the resistance movement. It was a strange situation to be working against her husband's side, but war is full of complications and contradictions like this, and she managed to keep her involvement secret from him. The reason for her involvement was her employer. She became devoted to him, especially as he now treated her like a daughter. He was antifascist, and she would run errands for him to sympathisers and safe houses that hid resistance fighters. She became all the more determined to help when she convinced herself that Marco had been killed. By this time, he was fighting against his former allies, and the German occupation of Venice had become more brutal. The Germans had poured over the Brenner Pass into the northern cities of Italy in order to become a full-time army of occupation. She came to the conclusion that Marco was dead when his letters (and money) stopped arriving from wherever he was stationed.

She therefore became all the more determined to do her bit for the resistance movement. So when a beautiful, smiling young woman carrying a hand basket of fruit and groceries walked across the Piazza San Marco, the German soldiers looked at her, not what was in the basket. If they had emptied the basket onto the ground in the square, inside it they would have seen a false compartment that could hold a handgun and clips of ammunition. On the days when she was not carrying anything incriminating, she would sometimes stop and talk with them. She couldn't speak much German but they knew enough Italian to keep her interested. There was the usual banter about meeting up after the war and offers to take her back to Germany when all of this was over—they were the words that come out of the mouths of lonely and bored soldiers. When there was no officer around, they would give her a cheery wave, to which she always responded.

By being able to hide her contempt for the army of occupation, she was of great assistance to the resistance movement because she was able to beat the night-time curfew, and the Germans never suspected her of anything. Her friendliness with the German soldiers was misunderstood by some of the local population, who would spit at her and call her names. They didn't know any better, and she felt this also assisted the deception, so she didn't worry about it. Her basket was never searched by the admiring soldiers on duty. In addition, important messages were slipped into her clothing, the lining of her brassiere being the favourite hiding place.

On one such occasion when she reached a safe house, she set down her basket and un-self-consciously pulled down the top of her dress and removed her brassiere in order to extract the message. This action caused her full breasts to be completely exposed. The jaw of the young resistance man who witnessed these unexpectedly treats dropped open. Her breasts were just a bit too large to be described as beautiful, but notwithstanding that, they were a sight for sore eyes. This lack of self-consciousness didn't matter to Isabella, because three years of wartime conditions had changed her from a naïve young girl into a brave young woman who did not stand on any kind of ceremony.

"What's the matter with you?" she barked at him. "Never seen a naked woman before?" The young man, Angelo Carlucci, was stunned but was able to compose himself enough to give a satisfactory response.

"Yes I have, but never one so beautiful, Signorina."

"It's not Signorina, it's Signora. My husband is with the partisans somewhere in Sicily, fighting the Germans, and is most likely dead by now. So what do you think of that?" In her anger she still she made no attempt to cover her naked breasts.

Angelo was not to be bullied by the sharpness of her tongue or her defiance, no matter how stunning this young woman was. "There is little that I can say, Signora, other than the fact that I guess that he fought for Il Duce before changing sides. I am glad he did—change sides, I mean. Fighting for Il Duce is something that I refused to do, so I do this instead. I apologise if my comments offend you in any way, and I hope you may soon have positive news from him. It must be very worrying for you."

She ignored what he had to say and passed over the piece of paper removed from her brassiere, her breasts swaying as she turned. "Here, take this, I don't know what it says but I am told that I must say one word to you, and it is *laguna*. I hope it means something to you because it means absolutely nothing to me." He nodded without being able to take his eyes off her as she redressed the top half of her body. "Now that you've finished staring at me, I'll be on my way. It would be a good idea in future if instead of gawping at me you emptied the basket that I have risked my life bringing to you. You still haven't done it." Her eyes flared with anger.

"Forgive my rudeness, Signora. I was very much distracted, and I will do better the next time you visit, which I hope is soon." This leaden gallantry got what it deserved as she picked up the now emptied basket.

"If we are both still alive, I suppose that is a possibility. Now, do you have anything that I must return with?" She buttoned up her dress.

"Yes, I must find it upstairs."

"Find it? Why are you so completely unprepared for my visit?" There was no answer to this question. He returned from upstairs with a piece of paper. She looked at him with a pained expression on her face. Hiding the message would mean undressing again. "This time you can look away." He turned his back, only turning around when she spoke again. "*Allora*, it is time to go—*grazie, arrivederla, Signore*," she said formally, with an air of finality. He however was determined to have the last word. He was not supposed to give away his name but he did.

"It's Angelo, and ciao, Signora!" She closed the door behind her as she left without looking back. She realised that he had breached security by giving his name but decided to say nothing to anyone about it, inwardly acknowledging his attempt to be friendly.

Over the next few weeks, she got more accustomed to meeting with Angelo in one of the safe houses and, after a while, felt a tinge of disappointment when it was someone else on duty to take the latest delivery. By making discreet enquiries, she found out that Angelo was a key member of the resistance and that he had prevented the deportation of a number of Jewish children from their ghetto quarter in Venice by getting them out of the city undetected. Even at that stage, there were rumours about death camps in the German-occupied territories to the north beyond the mountains and east in places that Isabella had never realised existed let alone heard of.

The conversations they held became more cordial but very businesslike. When there was time, he invited her to sit down and talk, and she found herself dazzled by his great depth of knowledge and education. Her own education had been sparse, only improved by what her employer had taught her in the past three years. Angelo seemed like a teacher, explaining to her first the roots of the fascist movement and the need to fight against it. He said that he was a communist, something that had to be properly explained to her because she didn't know what it meant. His eyes blazed with excitement as he passed on news of Soviet victories on the Eastern Front. There, he said, was where the war would be decided. In Italy after the war, he declared, things would be different. Isabella was in no position to dispute any of what he said, even if she had wanted to.

After the first time, she no longer disrobed in front of him when retrieving messages from her clothing. Then he went missing for three weeks, and it was thought that he had been caught and perhaps shot after being tortured. But one day, he was there again. He was limping and had bruises on his face and body. He had been caught out at night, breaking the curfew. He got away without being shot because he could prove that he was a fisherman. He was able to explain that the weather had kept him at sea and delayed his arrival back in port. By that time, he was beyond the curfew hour but still had to get his fish over to the market. But reasonable excuse though it was, that didn't stop him from getting a good beating from the Gestapo as a warning, because the procedure was to immediately present yourself to the commandant at the port, and this he hadn't done. His excuse of having had no sleep for two days and therefore being exhausted to the point of forgetfulness was not accepted. Yes, he had been tired, and the story was good enough to convince the Gestapo, but what he had really been doing was delivering guns. Being a fisherman was just a cover story—the boats could move weapons around but ran the risk of being searched.

When he reappeared, on impulse, Isabella approached Angelo and kissed him lightly, as if acknowledging his bravery and suffering. Standing back from him, she said what she had been meaning to say for some time:

"I want to apologise to you for the way I behaved when we first met. It was wrong of me to show no modesty but you shouldn't have stared so much. It was rude of you but I also showed you no respect. You notice that when I come here now I behave in the correct manner, and that is the way it should be."

Angelo smiled, touching the area of his face where she had kissed him. He judged that it would not be a good idea to say how much he had enjoyed their first encounter; as far as he was concerned, she could undress in front of him again any time she liked. "If you say so, Isabella," he answered (it was the first time that he had called her that) and he continued, "but neither of us should be ashamed." Then he went over and lightly kissed her on the cheek. "Now we are even."

Isabella flushed when she felt the contact against her skin, turned, and left. He had found out her name, which on reflection was again bad security. She wondered how he found out, and it occurred to her that he must have made enquiries about her.

Still with no word from Marco, Isabella now believed that he was dead. She and Angelo became lovers and remained so until Marco's unexpected return a few months later. Isabella was shocked to see Marco again and, in truth, not a little disappointed because Angelo had been a gentle and considerate lover, whereas Marco liked to satisfy his lust without consideration of his partner's needs. When during a row these feeling became evident,

Marco completely lost control and exerted his rights over her in the most brutal of ways, as was his wont.

When Angelo heard the news of her husband's return, like the experienced resistance man he was, he just faded away into the background, and Isabella neither saw nor heard from him again.

When Marco heard about the affair, he said he was going to find Angelo and kill him. "What is his name?" he demanded.

"I only know him by his code name," she lied.

"And what is that?"

Isabella said the first thing that came into her head, remembering their first ever encounter. "*Laguna*."

"I will get my friends to find out who he was!"

When Marco returned home after the war, he tried for a long time to discover the identity of this man and found out that there was no one who used this code name in the resistance movement. After drawing yet another blank, Marco came home in a foul temper. It was dinnertime, and through mouthfuls of pasta, he once again angrily confronted Isabella, but she still maintained that this was his name. She told him over and over again that it was forbidden for people in the resistance to know the real names and identities of comrades. Marco was not impressed.

"You sleep with a man and you don't even know his name! What kind of woman are you? I risked my life to come and see you under the noses of the Germans but what did you care?"

"I was a lonely woman who thought that you were dead. And now, Marco, tell me the names of all the girls you went with while you were away—I hear there were many." There was silence, and he looked away from the angry fire in her eyes. "So, what kind of man does that make you?"

Isabella picked up the bowl containing what was left of the pasta and emptied it over his head before storming out into the warm night air. As the years went by, there were frequent rows like this, and that seemed to be one of the features of my childhood.

CHAPTER 3

EARLY YEARS

Italy, my country—originally loyal to Germany during the Second World War—saw the error of its ways, changed its allegiance, and ended up on the winning side; I suppose there is some honour in that. But we had managed to earn the contempt of many nations in the world during the post-war period, which was a terrible time of austerity and deprivation. We had Mussolini and the tide of nationalism to thank for this misfortune.

It was during the First World War that Winston Churchill, no less, had called my country the harlot of Europe because of its territorial ambitions and willingness to make an alliance with any power block that would agree to its political aims and desire for new lands. After the Second World War, it was not surprising that things changed completely and there was a determination not to repeat the mistakes of the inter-war years. My country voted to become a republic, and there followed a long series of coalition governments. Our reputation now was not for firm government but for political instability. As we emerged from the war, our detractors still painted us as unreliable and cowardly. I know that many people in Britain still hold these views, even today. These opinions are mostly held by the older generation that fought in the war but get passed down to the next, then the next, and so it goes on.

The same feeling is expressed in Britain against the Germans, with a much greater degree of justification. However, in Britain it always seems to be accompanied by bad impersonations based on the way Germans, particularly Nazis, are portrayed in Hollywood war films. My English husband says it is part of the British psyche to do this, and it is so ingrained that it is impossible to avoid this stereotyping of people. I don't accept this explanation and just think that it is another form of racism. We don't now go to England very often, but it gets a bit tiresome when people you are introduced to automatically think because you are Italian you must work in the restaurant trade or know someone connected with Mafia. It is quite insulting, and even when it is done in fun, I find my sense of humour deserting me. You find people making these sorts of jokes as if it is the first time you have heard them. Having given offence, they then say, "No offence intended," or "Only a joke!" Then they seem to want you to go on talking to them as if nothing has been said that might have upset you. I wonder if they realise how stupid this makes them look (or perhaps it is me getting more and more sensitive as I grow older).

After the war, the district where I lived in Venice was far enough away from the developments on the mainland, in industrial Marghera and Mestre, so it was the surrounding lagoon rather than the city that was changing. Here the speed of building was much in line with the other industrial regions of northern Italy, so Venice as a city within this area turned to face the mainland rather than resist the tireless march to the future, as it had done in the two previous decades. There were benefits from this, and it meant that my parents always had work, even if it meant sometimes crossing the causeway over to the mainland. Despite the hard conditions, we never went without what was necessary to sustain us, although it must have been harder initially for Gianna than it was for me. I had her clothes when she grew out of them, and Mamma never wasted food or threw away anything that could be used again. I have to say that I never felt deprived and just accepted it if we could not afford things.

I was lucky in that Gianna was a kind and loving elder sister, and far from being jealous, I worshipped her, hanging on her every word and deed. She was my role model, and I would try and imitate everything she did. In looks, I grew up into a younger version of her, which was something to be thankful for. In those early years, I can never remember her getting into trouble or there being any rows or shouting matches in the home that involved her. Papa was this shadowy figure who was never around much—always away working during the week and, when home at the weekends, nearly always asleep before or after drinking sessions. It was Mamma, Gianna, and I who did things as a family, and we spent many happy days out on the Lido, from where we witnessed the comings and goings in the lagoon as we played at the water's edge. I can't remember Papa being with us on any of these occasions but that might be my memory being deliberately selective.

And indeed, as Gianna and I grew up, another of the features of our childhood and early teenage years was the constant work that seemed to be going on there in the lagoon. The fathers of our school friends worked on many of the construction projects, and we would overhear conversations that they would have with my father when he met up with them. There was a huge sense of unease that the lagoon was being damaged by the ever increasing flow of merchant ships and the pollution from the new industrial developments, which was killing some of the fish. It was also felt that the creation of artificial islands by draining areas of the marsh, together with the establishment of large fish farms, was upsetting the tidal and ecological balance within the lagoon. By the time I was old enough to really understand, in the early 1960s, a deeper channel was dredged from Malamocco to Marghera, in order to allow big oil tankers to reach port. There were lots of objections and dire warnings about this but it still went ahead. The wise old heads who knew about the lagoon were not exactly ignored, but their objections were overridden in the name of progress.

All of this did not seem to matter too much to two young girls. All that we cared about was that the smaller boats and water buses ran around the lagoon and that the sun was shining (or that it was at least dry on those days when we planned to go out). What really changed our lives was when Mamma became sick. It was late summer, and I suppose I was ten when I remember Gianna telling me that Mamma had to go to the hospital. This was the start of her long struggle against cancer.

Papa did not receive the news calmly or react very well to the situation. It was the first time I saw Gianna get really angry with Papa, when Mamma took to her bed after a morning of feeling faint and sick after some treatment she had undergone at the hospital the previous day. Papa seemed to have no patience. By now it was early September, and the next day Gianna took over in the kitchen to make Sunday lunch. It took longer than if Mamma was doing it, but it turned out really nice (not that Papa showed much appreciation).

She said sarcastically, "It must be really inconvenient for you to have to wait for your lunch, Papa. Don't worry; I will get Luisa to help me with the dishes, as I know you won't have time to give me any assistance." The late arrival of the meal had meant that he had not been able to get out in time to go and see the opening game of the football season. He went out anyway, clearly still in a bad mood that his afternoon had been disrupted. I helped Gianna with the dishes but noticed that tears had filled her eyes. This made me cry too. I went up to her and hugged her, and we comforted each other.

The treatment that Mamma was getting went on for an extended period, during which time she was often very weak. She had major surgery to have a kidney removed because the cancer had spread. Papa was never around, and it was left to Gianna to nurse Mamma nearly all of the time, helping her to do the simple things like getting in and out of the bath and dressing her. At that stage, she was also looking after me. Papa would not let his own mother come and assist us because of his dislike for her second husband. I was to later discover that his mother was petrified of Papa and his moods. The basis for this was that he had physically threatened her on a number of occasions, mostly after he had been drinking. Gianna also said that for grandmother, it provided a good excuse for not coming over, as she was not especially close to her daughter-in-law either.

Gianna impressed upon me the need to learn how to do certain things for myself and then do them without being asked, and under her supervision, I learned very quickly. This degree of self-reliance has stayed with me all of my life. The legacy of this was that it meant that my first husband turned into a man who relied upon me to do everything and therefore did very little for himself. And indeed, when I married for the second time, one of things that I found difficult to get used to was my new husband who helped around the house and was good at do-it-yourself projects. Suddenly, there was someone who could mend things when they broke or diagnose problems if anything went wrong and then knew what to do about it.

How Gianna managed at the time, I simply don't know. Taps dripped, doors wouldn't shut, lights would not switch on, and appliances failed, but Gianna found people who would come and sort things out. Papa hardly noticed, apart from complaining about the bills when they arrived. At school, she was brilliant, top of her class in nearly every subject and the envy of her peers. She was particularly good at languages, and there were girls who envied her looks and wanted to be like her.

She attracted the attention of the boys but brushed them off without fuss and with no interest, as if they didn't exist. One lovesick boy was infatuated with her, and on finding out that I was her younger sister, he passed me a note to give to her. I thought this was quite exciting, and it must have sounded so in my voice: "Here is a letter for you from a boy, Gianna; he said his name is Pietro." Gianna took it from me, looking at the writing on the envelope, but appeared not to be impressed. There was a flicker of annoyance showing in her face as she spoke.

"In which case it will be the same as the other three he has sent me." Gianna opened the bin and threw the letter in unopened and continued with making the dinner. I was surprised at this and thought Pietro would be angry. This story doesn't end there. The ever-persistent Pietro approached me again at school, still desperate for my sister to speak with him. He told me that he was so unhappy when Gianna did not reply. He revealed in dramatic fashion that he even contemplated suicide. He begged me to speak to Gianna, and feeling sorry for him, I said I would try. That evening, I approached my sister whilst she was busy doing some work.

"Pietro says he is going to kill himself if you won't speak to him."

At this news, Gianna's brow furrowed and she set her pen down on the desk.

"It's wrong of him to pester you with his stupid talk. In any case, those who threaten to do that kind of thing never carry it through—he just wants attention." She decided to make light of it as she considered the alternatives that were open to Pietro. "If he really means what he says and does go through with it, then at least there are three bridges to choose from: Ponte dell'Accademia, Ponte degli Scalzi by the station, or better still the Rialto, where his body will sure to come in contact with a passing vaporetto. That will make a mess." It was said in a very mater-of-fact tone, and I suppose that is what made me laugh, and she started too.

I suggested, "What about jumping off the Campanile in San Marco?"

"Yes, even better—he should do it when there are lots of people around!" Now her mood changed. "Luisa, don't let him bother you anymore; he can try and talk to me directly if he wants to, not that it will do him any good."

And that is what did happen. I made an effort to contact Pietro and told him that Gianna might speak to him if he approached her, but no more notes please. I don't know how he found out where we lived, because I didn't tell him, but I guess he asked one of the children of our neighbours or, worse still, perhaps he stalked Gianna or me. One Saturday morning, he turned up at our apartment in Cannaregio and rang the bell. Over the intercom, I heard him say that he had come to see Gianna. There was little expression in her voice as she let him in. She made sure that she kept him in the hallway, no more than a metre away from the door. "What is it you want to say to me, Pietro?"

Pietro had probably been rehearsing what he was going to say many times over—now his moment had finally come. I listened in to the conversation from behind the kitchen door, which was open just enough for me to hear the exchange. "Gianna, I have stopped sending you notes. My Papa says that this is a stupid way to behave toward a woman, and he is right. I have come to ask you to go out with me and would like to invite you to my house for dinner some day very soon, and then you can meet my parents. It will be a nice day for all of us. It has taken a lot of courage for me to do this, and I have walked from where I live in San Lorenzo to ask you. What is your answer?"

Poor Pietro—this sounded rehearsed, very stilted and formal, but I suppose I had to admire his courage. He was probably dying in his shoes as he stood there waiting on the words of the goddess he had created in his own mind. Gianna listened to the speech and replied, "Firstly, Pietro, I must thank you for stopping the notes. Trying to speak to me through my younger sister was a very dumb thing to do. I think that you are at heart a very nice boy, and it is flattering that you should write such nice things. Secondly, you need to know the reason that I am not interested in going out with you or any other boy is because *sono una lesbica*. This may come as a surprise to you. Thirdly, if I find out that you have divulged the details of our private conversation to anybody, I will kick you in the balls. Is that clear? Now I must wish you a good day and ask you to leave because I have a lot of work to do."

And with that, I heard the door close and Pietro no doubt slipped off disconsolately back to San Lorenzo. All that way just to be rejected; I couldn't help feeling that Gianna could have been a bit nicer, but I suppose she didn't want to give him any encouragement at all. It was a brutal rejection. His facial expression as he took in Gianna's reply had gone from delight to dismay and then shock. I had heard girls in my class at school whispering about lesbians but I did not yet know for sure what one was. I immediately went and looked it up in my dictionary. I read what it said but still didn't understand. Asking Gianna was out of the question because I didn't want her to know that I was listening to her conversation with the luckless Pietro.

CHAPTER 4

VIOLATIONS

Gianna was making her way home, alone, from the hospital, on foot as usual. She had not been able to stay long because it was one of those days when Mamma was sick and the nurses advised her to leave. She was not far from home when two boys she recognised from school, but did not know by name, stepped out from one of the *calle* and pushed her into the recess of a doorway. The larger of the two gripped her arms and pushed her flat against the wall with his face close to hers. She could feel his breath upon her face, and it smelt of stale tobacco and garlic. His face was very close to hers as he spoke. "We know your secret, *lesbo,* and we don't like *lesbos*." Whilst she was immobilised, the other knelt down, put his hands up her skirt, and pulled down her knickers to her ankles; he stood up again. "So just watch your step, *lesbo,* or you will get more than you bargained for." Then he spat in her face before giving her a final shove against the wall and walking casually off with his accomplice in the opposite direction from where she was going. She could hear their laughter fading away in the distance.

Gianna felt stunned and humiliated as she reached down to pull up her knickers and wiped the spittle from her face and her now dishevelled hair. It was revolting. She considered herself quite tough but started to cry when she got home. Only one person could have been responsible for this. The once lovesick Pietro had turned vengeful because of the rejection he had been dealt. What bothered Gianna most of all was that her two persecutors would not finish at that one encounter, and there was the threat that they would be looking to trouble her again in future.

At school, she continued to get threatening and abusive notes and suspected that it was Pietro and his friends because of the frequent taunting that also went on. She realised that it was a huge mistake to give out details about her sexuality to Pietro. She thought that it would end his interest in her, but all it did was give ammunition to people who did not like her. She made no attempt to confront her tormentors, who were frustrated by her lack of reaction.

She didn't bother to report it, even when one day one of the boys, egged on by the other, indecently exposed himself as she was making her way home. She just looked away in disgust. Next, one of her textbooks went missing and when it turned up, there was an enlarged drawing, from memory quite a good one, it must be said, of the male sexual organs in an aroused state, stretching across the inside cover and flyleaf. The message written by the side of it was that Pietro loved her, though it wasn't in his handwriting. Gianna showed me this drawing just to indicate what she was up against. I had never seen a penis before. I rather stupidly said that I wondered if that was what Pietro was really like. Quick as a flash, Gianna answered that she didn't think so but it is the way he would like to be, and I laughed.

"Are you going to do anything about this?" I asked, to which she replied no, only wait until they got bored and stopped.

On yet another return journey from the hospital, she saw the same two boys hanging around, and this time Pietro was with them. Luckily, she noticed them before they spotted her, and she was able to find another way home, always looking about her in case they suddenly appeared from somewhere out of the shadows. The continuing threat now receded in her mind, but she was attacked again after a particularly distressing visit to hospital. She had also been surprised by the presence at visiting time of grandmother, who asked Gianna not to mention to Papa that she had been to see Mamma. It was at night and her guard was down, as she was buried deep in thought. This time, the assault was more physical as she was pushed into a blind *calle*. It felt like the hands of both boys were all over her body. Pietro stood at the end of the *calle* as lookout whilst the other two set to work.

The same boy who had spat on her spoke directly into her face as he had done before, his breath still reeking of stale tobacco and garlic. "This time, we're gonna see what you've got, *lesbo*!" Now they were laughing and pulled her dress up over her head and tore it off. She was overwhelmed and powerless. They soon had her completely stripped and down on the ground. One pinned her to the ground and forced his tongue inside her mouth whilst the other dropped his trousers and underpants. He knelt down, parted her legs with his knee, and tried to force his penis into her. His accomplice made room for him, and he now clamped his hand over her mouth to muffle her screams. He called to Pietro to get himself ready because he was next. "By the way," he said, now looking down at her, "nice tits." His partner was unable to force his way in because Gianna would not keep still. "Hurry up, can't you? I want a piece before someone comes along."

"Well, give her a good slap or bang her head on the ground to stop her moving or I won't be able to fuck her."

"Don't hurt her too much!" shouted Pietro with growing anxiety, his eyes moving quickly from the street to the alley and back again.

Garlic-and-Stale-Tobacco-Breath partially relaxed his grip in order to find another way of subduing Gianna, and as he did, she managed to bite his hand that was over her mouth, causing him to yelp with the pain and draw back. As the blood oozed from his hand, she squirmed away from the other one, who still had not been successful in trying to penetrate her, and then her continuous screaming and calls for help frightened them all off.

"Someone's coming!" shouted Pietro. They started to panic and quickly ran off, with her unsuccessful attacker falling over as he tried to pull his trousers up over his fully aroused penis.

"Wait for me, you fuckers," she heard him cry out, and after they had gone, she lay on the ground for a few seconds in shock, unable to cry. Gradually, she started to put back on her partly torn and now soiled clothing. A man and a woman came past, and she called to them from the shadows. They stopped and immediately saw what had happened to her. She told them most of the story. They took her to their nearby home, and she cleaned herself up with the help of the lady whilst the man telephoned the police. They urged her to go to the police station, which she duly did, and the couple were good enough to accompany her in the launch. Gianna telephoned me from the main Questura and told me not to worry because she was going to be late home; she wouldn't explain why she was there, and I was worried that she had done something wrong. The police launch took them all home afterwards, and the officer saw her to her door, checking to make sure she would not be alone.

When she arrived inside, she told me what happened. I was horrified, particularly at how she looked. There was a trace of blood from her nose, and her arms and legs had scratches and scrapes all over. She also had a black eye. The police inspector who interviewed her had persuaded her to tell him the full story. She started at the beginning, telling him all of the background, even volunteering details about her sexual preference. This was going to have serious repercussions for Pietro and his friends, as the incident leading directly back to them was undeniable.

The next day, the police launch called and took us to school, which made me feel important despite the fact that the situation was clearly a very grave one. By the time we arrived, the *Commissario* of the Questura was already in discussion with the head teacher and other officials. At school Pietro, who had already been named, and the other two culprits were quickly and easily identified by Gianna. The subsequent investigation led to all three of them admitting that they were there when the incident took place. They were not charged with assault, as it was her word against theirs. They insisted she had arranged to meet them and she wanted sex with all of them but changed her mind at the last moment, became hysterical, and started screaming. The torn clothing was explained away by one of the boys, saying he got a bit excited because she was egging him on.

The story was scarcely believable but they got away with it despite the fact that Gianna had scratches and bruises that were clearly visible. Their parents were made to go to the Questura, and the Commissario made it clear that the only reason they were not being charged was because there were no witnesses. All they got was a suspension for two weeks from school for unruly behaviour. One particularly stupid policeman warned Gianna about the dangers of going home unaccompanied. It was almost as if he accepted the word of the three boys. He looked embarrassed after she said that she had to make almost nightly visits to our sick mother, who was in hospital suffering from cancer. The three boys were made to agree that they would not harass Gianna any more. Only Pietro showed any sign of remorse. He was scared to go near her and sent one of his pathetic notes that said he was really sorry and wouldn't trouble her ever again.

After they started serving their suspension, the nasty talk still circulated around the school, which had repercussions for Gianna because the details of her being a lesbian became even more widely known. This invited all kinds of name-calling from people in her peer group, some of whom used to be friendly but who now turned against her. It was as if all the pent-up jealousies over the years were coming out and they wanted a reason to dislike her. It showed great mental strength that she was able to rise above it. Not everyone had a problem with Gianna being gay. She attracted the attention of some older girls who became her friends, as well as two who remained intensely loyal from within her own peer group.

Although I was previously unsure, I quickly found out from the girls in my class what a lesbian was and received many taunts from those who sided with the suspended boys: "What's it like to have a sister who fucks with girls? Does your sister fuck you as well, little lesbo?" I found all of this very upsetting, and I was reduced to tears on a couple of occasions by my tormentors. Luckily, my teachers picked up on what was going on and were very kind to me. They quietly confronted the bullies, and the unpleasantness stopped. Well, on the surface it did, but I received a number of lewd notes and disgusting drawings. Eventually, it ceased but only after the whole affair had played itself out a few months later.

These events were concealed from Mamma, who never knew anything about the bother we had been in until well after it was over. Gianna managed to disguise the full nature of what had happened; otherwise, it would have upset her even more than it did. However, Papa did find out the full story. He managed to keep a level head and went to the school and the Questura to be put fully in the position. He insisted on being present when the Commissario handed out his lecture to the families. Gianna said it was difficult to know what concerned him more, the bullying and attempted rape or the shocking revelation about her sexuality. He didn't know how to properly discuss it with her but murmured that these people were not going to get away with what they had done. He was outraged that the perpetrators had gotten off so lightly, and he said was going to even things up. "They didn't look like they were very sorry to me," he said, "and I certainly didn't hear them say it. I'll *make* them sorry." I thought at the time that it was just Papa and his big talk. "I've still got friends in this town," he said menacingly. Even this sounded a bit feeble to me.

But it was a fact that he did still have friends that could mostly be traced back to his days in the army. He was a proud member of a veterans association, a few of whom were old comrades that he still went drinking with. I have to say that one or two of them looked like very rough types, and whenever I saw them, they used very bad language. They were the crudest types imaginable. A couple of nights later, Papa came back from drinking in his favourite bar, still going on about the attackers, and said, "We'll see about them, don't you worry."

Just when the heat was starting to die down, the boy who was responsible for holding Gianna down, and whose hand she bit, disappeared the second Saturday night of three into his period of suspension from school. Two days later, his fully clothed body was fished out of the Grand Canal quite near to the Rialto Bridge. It had become trapped under a stationary vaporetto that had been moored up for the night. The autopsy revealed that he had been drinking, enough to suggest that he was very drunk, but did he fall or was he pushed? According to the forensic pathologist, he was certainly alive before he went into the water, but it was not possible to tell if it was homicide. Apart from what he did to my sister, the boy was a known troublemaker and bully, so whilst there was a huge sense of shock, it could not mask the fact that many of his peer group felt that he had gotten what he deserved no matter how it had happened. Papa telephoned a couple of days later, ostensibly to find out how we were.

This was unusual for him. I excitedly told him that one of the boys who attacked Gianna was dead, drowned in the Canal near the Rialto.

"Good riddance to bad rubbish," was all that he said in a dull, flat tone before asking to speak to my sister. According to Gianna, he did not sound in any way shocked or surprised. He gave her a telephone number to contact if there was any further trouble.

Then another mystery took place exactly two weeks later. The boy who had unsuccessfully tried to force his way inside Gianna during the course of the attack never returned from a Saturday night out in Lido de Jesolo, which is a place where a lot of young people go to find the clubs that simply do not exist in Venice. Before his disappearance, he had finished his suspension and was back at school. He was still upset about his friend's death and started mouthing stuff about it being all Gianna's fault and saying that he was going to get her. He also went about saying that the reason he had not been able to get up inside the lesbo was that his penis was too big for her narrow little lesbo fanny, but next time it would be different. "I'll have her moaning, squealing, and begging for mercy as I ram it up her." This threatening behaviour and foul-mouthed talk was made known to the school authorities as well as Papa, who sensed danger and made arrangements to come home as soon as possible.

Papa called in to see the Commissario of the Questura. The boy was reported to the police and brought in for questioning, accompanied by his parents. As it happened, a number of witnesses came forward at school as well when he was issuing his threats, and he ended up being immediately expelled. The police applied to the court for a restraining order, and it was granted. He was forbidden to go anywhere near Gianna. Papa seemed happy about this and decided to return to work, but not before he had spent a lot of time talking on the telephone. He was annoyed that the boy's parents behaved in a totally passive manner all the way through the session down at the Questura and that there had been no trace of apology toward our family, even when the Commissario invited them to say something. I didn't know who it was Papa was speaking to on the telephone, we thought perhaps it was a lawyer, but he left us quite content that everything was in order. "There is nothing to worry about. It is all taken care of." We thought he meant that the police had matters under control.

The full details of the restraining order placed on the boy laid down that he was not allowed anywhere near Cannaregio and could not leave town and had to report to the Questura every evening at 8:00 PM. He complied with this for a few days but in the end, he disobeyed this, of course. He cleared off on the Saturday night without checking in. His two friends who had been out with him at the same club said that they were all very drunk and their friend had been sick a couple of times that evening. Apparently, he had gone out again for a third time for some fresh air but hadn't returned. His body never turned up, as far as I know.

Some people were starting to put two and two together, but there was no police investigation into the possible link with the attempted rape of my sister by him and the other deceased boy. To the police, he was just another known troublemaker, and not too many tears were being shed outside of the bereaved family. Another thing to remember here was that with no body recovered, there was no actual confirmation that he was dead yet; the police classified him as missing. It was possible that he had just run away or had gotten lost and might turn up later. A missing person file was opened at the Questura, and posters started to appear. Some of these were defaced and had the word *rapist* scrawled across them, and rather sinisterly, *already dead* was written across others.

My sister and I did not know what to think, and these events became the talk of the school. In the end, the teachers got fed up with the students being so distracted and continuously speculating about what may have taken place. They decided to forbid any further discussion of it. The speculation continued nonetheless, only not within earshot of the teachers. After a couple of days, grim jokes started to circulate, and some boys started to tease Pietro with a number of comments: "Cheer up, Pietro, it's you next! Stay away from the canals. Watch your back! Fancy a trip to Jesolo this weekend?"

Pietro found none of this very funny. He was back from suspension by this time and had become a very subdued, almost haunted character. He looked sick. He certainly wasn't in the business of threatening anyone, and he went about his life at school with his head down, accompanied by two of his best friends who to me seemed to be acting as bodyguards. We were surprised when another note turned up at home for Gianna. She turned pale as she recognised the writing, and her stomach turned over as she opened it. It was from Pietro again, and I wondered what it was going to say. She read it to me out loud:

Dear Gianna,

I am very sorry for what happened and am deeply ashamed for the part I played in it. It was wrong of me and I hope that one day you will find it in your heart to forgive me. The other two boys, Luca and Fredo, are dead and I don't think either death was an accident. I can understand why you are still angry. Please don't have me killed. Remember I shouted out for them not to hurt you. I will do anything to make up for what I did and want to be your friend, please believe me.

Respectfully
Pietro

What a desperate letter! It struck me as rather pathetic. Gianna laughed but it was a harsh laugh that grated. Before she decided to show the note to Papa, she said to me that he should have confessed to the crime rather than say she wanted sex with all of them. And as for not wanting her to be hurt, he was next in the queue to rape her had they not been scared off.

Papa came home again shortly after the second boy had gone missing. When we told him that the second boy had not yet been found, he said that he was not surprised and shrugged his shoulders.

"Do you think that he is dead, Papa?"

"How long has he been missing?"

"Three days."

He nodded. "Then I think he is probably dead by now. Beyond forty-eight hours, then, there is little prospect of him still being alive."

"What do you think happened?"

"I have no idea—he might have drowned like his mate. I don't care, to tell you the truth. He is the type who always breaks the rules. First he tries to rape your sister; then he makes more threats; then he disobeys the police; then he ends up missing. Why should anyone be surprised?"

He showed no emotion whatsoever regarding the note either but kept it just the same. Gianna asked him what he was going to do with it. "The letter is trash written by someone who is trash. Now he's sorry but it is far too late for that. So there is only one place to put this trash, and that is in the trash bin." When Gianna looked for it in the bin later on, it was not there, so it was obvious to her that Papa had kept it.

Now the final part of the story: two weeks later, Pietro was set upon one night and savagely beaten up in San Lorenzo, near where he lived, and so bad were his injuries that he ended up in hospital in a coma. There were no witnesses, or at least no one came forward with any information. After three weeks, the doctors turned off the life support machine that was keeping him alive. He never regained consciousness. His head had been banged repeatedly against the ground during the assault, and his genitals had been stamped upon several times. The sense of shock in my school was now huge, and now it was no joking matter. People were genuinely scared. Gianna's tormentors were suddenly not so vociferous any more. It was very noticeable how students kept away from me and from Gianna. When they finally felt it was safe to approach me, I was asked by a number of students if my Papa had arranged for the boys to be done away with, to which I responded no, and that they should all grow up and just leave me and my sister alone.

Now, finally it was not lost on the police that all three of the boys who had been suspended for the attack on my sister were now either dead or missing. It seemed like some kind of Sicilian vendetta was being carried out in the normally trouble-free environs of Venice. The police somewhat belatedly decided to act, and Papa was questioned down at the Questura on three separate occasions. He had become a suspect but cooperated fully with them. He told them that it was a terrible tragedy and if he could help them, he would despite what the victims had tried to do to his daughter.

The second time he went to the Questura, he found himself sitting opposite the Commissario and two of his minions. This was a sign to him that the investigation was being stepped up. "Who do you think might have carried out these revenge killings, Signore Ambrosio? It is obvious that this is what they are. You are insistent that you played no part in them, but I am having trouble believing this."

"I simply don't know, Commissario." Papa was not going to volunteer any information unless pressed.

"Surely you must have some thoughts on who is carrying out vigilante-style killings in your name. Some of my officers have digging into your past. You are ex-army."

"Yes, I fought for my country—but that was a long time ago. In any case, what has that got to do with it?"

"You've not given me an answer to my question."

"I don't know who might have done it—perhaps there are a number of people who are outraged at what happened and the fact the boys were not formally charged. It was obvious what they tried to do to my daughter. The only people, it seems, who did not find it obvious were your officers—perhaps *they* didn't do so well, Commissario."

"Who might have been outraged?"

"Other parents of children at the school. If only the boys had admitted what they did and showed some remorse, then perhaps they would be alive today. When the system appears to fail, then this can drive people to do things they should not and take the law into their own hands."

"Including you?"

"I was not here, Commissario. I would not do such a thing, even though many would not blame me. I felt sorry for these boys that they should stoop to such a level. If you ask me, it is the parents that need to be held responsible. Why do parents allow their children to roam around out of control? Do you remember at the interviews that the parents never said a single word? It was as if my daughter was to blame. There was no apology—nothing. I have to work away but my daughters are always in by a reasonable time. My daughter visits her Mamma who is sick and she can't walk the streets safely—what are you going to do about it? The boy Pietro is attacked but there are no policemen anywhere at night time. Why?"

Papa continued to hold his nerve under questioning and only appeared to be alarmed when the Commissario indicated that we two girls were needed for questioning. When he came back after this interview, he told us that when we were questioned not to mention the note that Pietro had sent, under any circumstances. We did not ask why we should lie in this way. Both Gianna and I were subsequently interviewed separately to establish whether we knew anything, but in truth apart from the note and the threatening remarks made by my father when he was drunk, we knew nothing about the deaths.

We both played the dumb innocent role to perfection, and I suspect that Papa would have been proud of us. The police were very gentle with us, and we did not find the questioning at all intimidating. Papa was very keen to know how we got on and seemed relieved when we told him they didn't want to speak to us again just yet. There was nothing that the police could properly link with Papa to the deaths because he was away each time, and his alibis all checked out. He made very sure to be in company at the time when the acts of revenge were being carried out, and I figured he was forewarned. The investigation into the deaths made no progress whatsoever. One of his drinking pals eventually confided in me about his recollections at the time:

"One night, your Papa came into the bar when all the fuss over the boys had died down, and as usual he was shouting the odds. He was already half gone and buying everyone a drink. He shouted, 'Guess what, I have been down at the Questura and do you know all three of my daughter's attackers are now dead—and the police ask me, "What have you got to say?" and I say, "*Che peccato*!" and they let me go.'"

He never said, "*What a pity*" to us two girls, he merely reiterated what he said at the Questura—that the whole affair might have upset some other parents who also have young daughters and wanted to make sure that the three boys would never again trouble anyone. It was nothing to do with him, of course, and he also asked us rhetorically what he could do if people took the law into their own hands. As a family, we received a death threat, which was immediately reported to the police. It was easily traced back to the family of Pietro. His father was taken to court for this, and it was not without irony that his family and the family of the other two boys also started to receive death threats.

The police started to take an interest in Papa again but these threats could not be traced back to him or anyone else, even though they carried on for some time. Maybe it was old army friends of Papa taking it in turns to keep up the siege of the families. Gianna speculated that Papa was probably part of the new Venetian Mafia and would certainly have to do favours in return for what had happened. It was now very clear to us that he had arranged for all of the boys to be eliminated, even though he had not carried out the killings himself. That was something that we had to carry around forever, and I want to make it clear that I am not proud of this at all. Only recently I discovered that it was my father's ex-army comrades who had carried out the murders. The first boy had alcohol forced down his throat before being held down underneath the water. The second had been garrotted before his body was chopped up and taken out to sea in a fishing boat, where the pieces were thrown overboard. Pietro had been hunted down and set upon.

At last the heat died down after the death threats, but as a precaution we moved as a family from one part of Cannaregio to another. It was a much larger place than before, and we revelled in the extra space. One day, one of Gianna's girlfriends was visiting our new apartment. Papa, who was preparing to leave, came into my room.

Gesturing with his head in the direction of Gianna's room, he said, "Luisa, you must never be like that."

"Like what, Papa?" I knew by now what he meant but wanted to hear him say it.

"You know, preferring the girls." He exited in a hurry so as not to have to explain any further.

In the meantime, Mamma had responded quite well to treatment and appeared to be recovering. She found it difficult to adapt to her new surroundings at home but it was nice to have her back. It was a period that I later understood to be remission. Things did not appear to be going too well between her and Papa, and he continued to show his now customary lack of understanding. He refused to discuss the trouble that Gianna had been in with her, and as already stated, Gianna only told her the outline details. Mamma returned to hospital for more treatment, and on this occasion it coincided with one of Papa's infrequent spells at home. It was a Friday evening.

"And so how is my beautiful young daughter?" I remember him saying. These words poured forth from my father, who had quite clearly been drinking again. The words were directed at Gianna, not me. Gianna had prepared a very nice dinner, a little earlier than usual so that I could go out and meet some of my friends. I was stopping with them overnight and was very excited about it and therefore had no knowledge (until very recently) of what happened that evening after I left Gianna with my father.

After I left with my overnight bag, Gianna set about clearing away the dinner, not expecting any assistance from Papa. He sat at the table, watching her and drinking, getting more and more drunk as the evening went on. He got up and moved over toward the sink. He enveloped her from behind and said, "Ah, my beautiful daughter."

"Papa, please, I am busy and there is a lot to do before I go and see Mamma tomorrow." But he wouldn't let go and she continued to struggle.

"I am your Papa, and I love you so you must do as I say, especially as your Mamma and me cannot be together."

Gianna struggled to remove herself from his vice-like grip. "What are you talking about, Papa? Please get off and let me get on. You could help me instead of talking a load of drunken rubbish." Her hand pushed his face away but he spun her round and slapped her face so hard that she fell to the floor. He picked her up and slapped her again, pushing her toward the bedroom and throwing her onto the bed. It was then that he satisfied his vile lust not once, but twice in a frenzied manner whilst she was still semi unconscious from the blow that he had struck.

Later, he returned to the bedroom and said, "You must never tell your Mamma or your sister about this. What happened was wrong, but one thing it will do is cure you of this girl thing I keep hearing about, which is also unnatural. There is no need for it, do you hear me? You got yourself into trouble with those boys because of it, and I don't want any more trouble of that kind."

Gianna did not reply but just lay there, feeling the bruises on her face, aware of the sticky mess that she was lying in. She never told Mamma what happened, and I only found out when it turned up in her diary. She relived the trauma of it all in the pages of her diary over five years later. There were many references to the attack and how Papa had been like a wild beast. How could he have thought that what he did was a cure for her being a lesbian? These days, he would be classed as not only a violent criminal with psychopathic tendencies but also a totally unreconstructed individual. He was quite clearly capable of operating on only an incredibly simple level, which to me is a sign of a complete lack of basic education.

Back to the time of the terrible incident, I remember that I did not return from my overnight stay immediately. I was invited to stay an extra night, and when I telephoned home to ask whether it was possible, Gianna surprised me by saying it was allowed. Now it is easy to understand, because this gave her an extra day to recover from her trauma. By the time I returned, Papa had gone. I noticed the marks on her face and asked her what had happened, and she explained that she had been out and some boys, different ones from before, had picked on her.

"I knew this would happen," I cried out angrily. "Let's tell Papa and go to the police again."

But she said she couldn't be sure if she could recognise them again, as it happened when it was dark.

"Did they rape you?"

"No, they just smacked me about a bit. It was probably revenge for the boys who have been killed."

"Does Papa know?"

She had to improvise very quickly with her explanation.

"No, he had to leave soon after you—something to do with his work. I went with him to the station, and it happened on the way back."

I moved toward her and hugged her, and it was very noticeable that she wouldn't let me go as she was crying.

I loved my sister and couldn't stand to see her unhappy, and it started me crying as well.

"Don't tell Papa about this," she said, "he will only make a fuss like last time, and look what happened."

I have already rationalised how my father, being the type of man I have described, could have done this to her, but it was still especially cruel after what she had been through at the hands of her attackers just a few months before. It must have been very frightening for Gianna because she now knew that her father was a man with psychopathic tendencies as well as a sex maniac.

CHAPTER 5

Employment

From that time onwards, Gianna hardly spoke to Papa at all when he was there (which, as ever, was not very often). During one of his lengthy periods away, she set about cleaning the apartment from top to bottom, with me assisting her. She decided it would be a good idea to pull all the beds and furniture away from the walls and give the place a thorough spring clean. In my parents' bedroom, under the double bed, a number of boxes and a few folders were all gathering dust. It all needed sorting out and throwing away, as it looked as if it was no longer required. Papa had refused to throw anything away when we moved, but Gianna decided that it was time to make some more space. We decided to take a break for lunch before tackling this job. Gianna finished first and immediately got back to work a few minutes before me. When I tried to enter the room, the door appeared to be stuck. Gianna called out to me, "I can't let you in just yet, Luisa. I am moving things around. Come back in a few minutes."

This I did and noticed that she had put one box on the side; I moved toward it and started to look inside.

"Don't look in that one," she said. "It's not very nice." Too late—it was a box full of magazines and photographs.

"*Pornografia*," Gianna said by way of explanation, seeing that there was no point in trying to shield me from what was there. "Some of it is hideous; don't look at it, Luisa."

"What are you going to do with it?" I asked as I sorted through the first few on the pile; most of it was pictures of topless girls, but Gianna came over and sealed the box up before I could see too much more.

"I am going to throw it all away—it's disgusting stuff."

"Why does Papa buy it?"

"That's a good question but one that I advise you not to ask him. Some men are like that, I'm afraid."

I was deeply shocked but still curious. Before the refuse men took it all away, I sneaked a look at some of the material. The magazines were quite tame by modern-day standards, but there were individual photographs that were hard-core pornography. They were all black-and-white pictures of naked men and women lying on the bed. In some pictures, the sex act was taking place, and there were naked couples doing all manner of other things to one another, including bondage, anal sex, and oral sex. There were two women and one man; one woman and two men; two women together; two men together. Overall, it was deeply offensive stuff, and I was ashamed of myself for having looked at it. I didn't recognise any of the people in the photographs but wondered who would agree to take part in such disgusting poses. Some time later, I sensibly came to the conclusion that it was all for money and tried not to think about it. Gianna certainly didn't talk about it any more. It was taken away, and I wondered how soon Papa would miss it.

As I indicated previously, Gianna made friends with a few girls, two of whom she spent quite a lot of time with. Alessandra and Carla became regular visitors to the apartment and were very kind to me as well as being great friends with my sister. I never was aware of any gay activity taking place. On a couple of occasions, I saw them in a state of semi-undress but that was all. Only a couple of years later, when Carla's younger sister Anita tried to get me to sleep with her, did I find out that there was a rampant gay sect in existence amongst the girls.

I don't know what the turning point was but suddenly the girls stopped calling around as much, and Gianna was clearly focused on something else. One day, a very excited Gianna came home and told me that she had got a temporary job at the Galleria dell'Accademia and that she was leaving school. She was only seventeen and was advised not to do this before her studies were completed. She was a star pupil, and her teachers had great plans for her and predicted that she would go to University.

The school relented, however, when she explained the situation at home, with Mamma being in and out of hospital. She also said that she found it difficult to remain at school because of what had happened with the three boys. This had cast a shadow from which it was difficult to emerge. She explained that a large number of students believed that the boys had been murdered not just because of what happened to her but because she had wanted revenge. I can vouch for all of this because it didn't make my life very easy at school either. I was guilty by association in the eyes of some, despite the fact that I was only twelve years old when this all started and had, in effect, done nothing.

Gianna did not consult or tell Papa, who one day found out by chance. He didn't appear to care that she had given up her studies and was ready to accept that she was unhappy at school after what had happened. He was more interested in how much she was going to earn and said he hoped that she would be able to save some money for the future.

So Gianna started work. She was the office junior to begin with, and sometimes they asked her to do the boring job of sitting in the Galleria if one of the attendants was sick or on leave. She did this without complaining. She soon demonstrated that she was an enthusiastic and capable young woman who showed initiative. It also helped that she could speak German very well and English to a reasonable standard. Her bosses were impressed and quickly took to her, and she was given paid leave to go and improve her skills in both languages at a school in the nearby Dorsoduro district. Gianna absorbed learning like a sponge. I had chosen to learn German at school, and we had great fun speaking to each other in this language at home. She told me that it was a great way of me helping her.

The result for me at school was that I became the most fluent speaker of German. My teachers were dazzled by how proficient I had become. Gianna did not deliberately foster in me a hatred of my father, but it became clear to me that she held him in the greatest contempt. I assumed that it was all to do with his lack of attention to Mamma and those horrible photographs. When she suggested that we speak German even when he was home, I did not disagree. It used to drive him mad, as he simply did not know what was being said.

He ranted and raged, "I fought against the damned Germans in the war. I don't want to hear that spoken in this house. I forbid it!" But it made no difference.

"I believe you also fought with them," Gianna said, briefly lapsing back into her native tongue, "so why don't you understand any of the language?" She stood to attention, raised her right arm in the Nazi salute, and started singing in a loud voice:

"*Die Fahne hoch, die Reihen fest geschlossen,*
S. A. marschiert mit ruhig festem Schritt,
Kamraden …"

Papa held up his hand. "Enough!" he shouted.

She stopped but her disdain was obvious, and she drove the point home. "You must know that song, father, marching along with your Nazi German pals in the early years of the war."

He showed signs of losing his temper. "Yes, I remember it; every soldier knows the tune of the damned *Horst Wessel.* I didn't understand the words that they were singing, and in any case, I hated it."

"Well, conversing in German is an important part of my job, and it is also my way of helping Luisa with her studies. If you bothered to find out how she was doing at school, then you would know just how good she is—but you don't, do you? That's because you are hardly ever here."

I expected him to fly into a worse rage but he seemed cowed by this, almost afraid to respond. Instead, he did what he usually did when things were not going his way—he stormed out, found his favourite bar, and got drunk. I took my sister's side in everything because I now also resented how Papa behaved toward Mamma and her illness.

With Gianna making great progress at work, her bosses decided to give her more responsibility and got her to help with arranging the programme of exhibitions. The Galleria also used to lend out paintings as well, and she would come into contact with overseas visitors. On more than one occasion, an important and impressed visitor would say to the director of the Galleria, "Who is that young girl? Would she like to come and work with me for a while?" And the Galleria would guard its new asset very preciously and say she was not available.

A frequent visitor to Venice and the Galleria was a wealthy English art dealer who owned his own small gallery back in London and did freelance work for a number of major galleries in the United Kingdom. He was in his late twenties and had benefited from public school and University educations. He had managed a first class degree in art history. He was an expert on Italian art, particularly the Renaissance period. He was an easy-going, urbane Englishman, and his name was Charles Court. He, like many other visitors, was captivated by Gianna. But in his case, it went further because he fell in love with her. Gianna could easily be mistaken for a twenty-one-year-old, but in fact at this point in time, she was still only eighteen. Charles found this very difficult to believe and told her so as he was sitting opposite her, outside a café in the Campo de Carita, next to the Accademia vaporetto stop. He had invited her out to take coffee with him; it was late summer and still very warm. The light breeze brought the smell of her perfume over to him but could not quite mask the unpleasant smell that was coming off the waters of the Grand Canal. This was in the era before canal dredging took place on a large scale in the 1980s, which largely eliminated the problem.

"So you think I'm old," she teased. "Thank you for the compliment, Mr. Court."

"I didn't mean it like that," replied Charles, frantically backtracking and still searching for the right words. "I meant mature."

"What? *Maturo*, like a piece of ripe fruit?"

"No, no," he stammered, trying to search for the correct expression. "I wish I'd never started this."

Gianna thought she might help him out.

"Perhaps you mean an exquisite bottle of vintage Champagne, like the one you will drink tonight with your meal at the Gritti Palace."

"That's more like it." Charles was happy with any reference to wine, as he knew a lot about the subject. He reached for some words of inspiration and gleefully exclaimed, "You are like a fine bottle of *Veuve Cliquot*!"

"That means I am some kind of widow, doesn't it? So now I'm a mature widow? I am young and still single, in case you hadn't noticed."

"Oh God, I've made things worse, haven't I? I never knew you spoke French as well."

"Not really but I know enough to get by."

"Let me make amends for my clumsy talk. Join me tonight for dinner and we will drink a bottle of 'the widow.' That is what it is sometimes called in England."

But Gianna instantly looked down, shaking her head. "No, I must visit my Mamma, who is in hospital, and then I must get home and attend to my sister, who is only thirteen. Unless, of course, Mr. Court, you would like her to come to dinner as well?" Immediately his face fell, and she looked down again, pretending to be offended before speaking. "No, I thought not." It was a great act and she could tell that he didn't know he was still being teased. Charles was disarmed. His usual confidence seemed to evaporate when in the company of this young woman. Silence had descended. "Thank you for the coffee," she said as she got up to go back to the Galleria, and he quickly threw some lire on to the table and followed her, signalling to the waiter that he had left money on the table. They walked back in silence.

He stammered his way through an apology. "I am really sorry about your mother; I hope she gets better soon." He was annoyed with himself because he should have said this straight away when she mentioned her mother was in hospital.

"She won't—the doctors say she is terminal; it's just a question of time before she passes on." This also surprised him, and now inside, he was falling apart and couldn't think of anything to say at all, so she spoke instead, saying pleasantly to him, "Thank you once again, Mr. Court."

He left about one hour later and, as he departed, reflected that he had put up a less than an impressive performance in her company. He had just negotiated a good deal for the National Gallery in London with the director of the Galleria here in Venice, but he had got completely tongue-tied by a young girl, albeit one older than her years. He felt stupid and inadequate.

CHAPTER 6

DEATH IN THE FAMILY

Christmas came and went, and there was lots of fun and noise in our neighbourhood when the New Year arrived. There were fireworks going off outside but no one in our house was celebrating in the traditional sense, as we tended to Mamma, who spoke back to us with great difficulty through the pain barrier. "You girls should be out celebrating with your friends. Go on, I want you to go out and have some fun."

"No, Mamma," I remember Gianna saying. "We want to be with you. In any case, today is your birthday."

Well, let's face it, how could you go out and enjoy yourself in that situation? We took it in turns to be with Mamma, and Gianna had bought a small panetonne cake and put some extra icing on top with the number 40 as the centrepiece. Unfortunately, Mamma didn't manage to eat any of it, as she had no appetite. On the fifth of January, she gave up her long battle against cancer and died. The priest, who had been called when it seemed her time was at an end, arrived before she passed on, and he did his best to comfort us. Mamma had come home from hospital for Christmas and was still with us well beyond New Year, despite being very weak. For once, we were all there together as a family when she passed away, even Papa, who was absolutely distraught.

"Don't take any notice of him, Luisa," Gianna said in German. "He is either showing guilt or just feeling sorry for himself." Perhaps Gianna was being harsh but she went on to point out that he had contributed nothing to the festivities, apart from bringing in lots of bottles of drink, which were consumed only by himself. That fact was undeniable. When he went out of the room, she went on to impersonate him in his Venetian dialect: "She is dead, I am forty-two, what am I to do?" Being angry was Gianna's way of coping. I couldn't think of anything to say—I was just numb.

I couldn't be as hard as Gianna, and I went and comforted Papa whilst Gianna did all the practical things like telling relatives and arranging for the funeral to take place on the island of San Michele. When the day arrived, it was a sombre occasion; funerals are always this way, made worse by the fact that Mamma was so very young, only forty years old.

On the day of the funeral, we travelled over to the island of San Michele and Gianna stood well away from Papa, as if she didn't want to be contaminated by him. He was in the worst state. The boat returned to the city, nosing its way through the mist that hung over the lagoon that day. I looked over to Gianna and saw her go pale and shudder as she dealt with her own thoughts. Once she was off the boat, she was organising people and telling them what was going to happen next. This continued later on back at our apartment; she was the tower of strength that thanked everyone for coming. I helped her and made sure that everyone had something to eat and drink. On reflection, it was better to be occupied than just standing around.

I remember overhearing a number of mourners say to my Papa, "Marco, your girls are wonderful, you must be so proud of them. At least you still have them." These observations were very ironic indeed. He nodded through his tears, which poured out from very red eyes, but couldn't find any words to say. When everyone was gone, Gianna and I cleared away all the dishes and leftovers from the wake but Papa emerged from his bedroom only to go out to the bar.

Although we were very sad, Gianna and I did not cry when Mamma died. It had been, in any case, a very long good-bye, and we understood exactly what was going to happen and were ready for it. The doctors had explained everything and had made Mamma as comfortable as possible. To this day, I am so grateful that we were there when the end came and that she was at home. The main burden had fallen upon Gianna, so it was no wonder at eighteen that she appeared to be much older than her years. Relatives and family friends were very nice to us but disappeared after the funeral, and it was as if we ceased to exist. I suppose it is a human characteristic that people, including relatives, steer clear of bereaved families. Living beings have not yet learned how to deal with death, seemingly embarrassed by not knowing what to say.

The priest called around to see us again but Gianna made him feel very awkward. After he said he would like to see us regularly at Mass, she said that she could not be a hypocrite and would not attend. She explained that Mamma, a good person, had died so young and this had affected her deeply. She told him it had destroyed what little faith she had left. The priest did his best to explain these unfortunate circumstances away, but this did not make any impression upon my sister. She was in a combative mood. "I tell you what you can do, Father— you can pray for my dear Papa. At the moment, he is in a terrible state and feeling very sorry for himself now that my Mamma is dead. Whilst she was alive, he didn't seem to care very much when he was away enjoying himself with other women and trying to act the big man that he will never be. However, you can have the job of forgiving him because I never shall."

The priest decided it was time to retreat, still vowing to pray for her, hoping that she would see things differently in time.

"I don't think so, Father."

"I will still pray for your Papa, as you have asked. Please get him to come and see me when he is next at home."

"I can't do that—I don't speak to him about such matters any more." I was cringing with embarrassment and decided it was time to intervene. After the treatment that Gianna meted out to the priest, I now knew perhaps this was the reason people stayed away from grieving families. He was only doing his best, after all, and I took pity on him.

"I will, Father. When I see him I will tell him." Thankfully, the priest then went but not before I took in his smile of gratitude.

In the spring, Charles Court arrived back in Venice, not on business but on vacation. He called in at the

Galleria and greeted everyone cheerily and asked where Gianna was. The tone of his voice tried to hide that this was an incidental enquiry and that she was not the main reason for his visit, as indeed she was. He found out. Apparently, she was at a meeting but would be out from it soon. He decided to wait and killed the time by walking around the lower floor rooms of the Galleria. He was just thinking about going back to the office to ask again, when suddenly she was there. A light voice quiet in tone came from behind him. "*Buongiorno, Signore Court.*"

He turned around quickly to see Gianna standing there, even more beautiful than he remembered. "Well, hello there, Gianna. First of all, how is your mother?"

Gianna replied in English in a very level tone, "She is dead, Mr. Court. She passed away about four months ago on the fifth of January."

This was the most terrible start of a conversation for Charles, in fact the worst imaginable. "I am so terribly sorry, I didn't know."

Gianna viewed him coolly before replying in a considered tone, "Well, you were not on the list of people that I felt I had to notify, and of course I haven't heard from you since the last time you were in Venice."

This was a barbed comment if ever there was one. Momentarily he deflected it. "I hope she did not suffer."

Gianna was not in the mood for letting him get away with this polite riposte. "The fact is, she did suffer, I'm afraid. It was a long and painful death."

"I am so sorry; cancer is terrible and so little can be done it seems." He paused and when there was no response, he continued, "I wish I had been on your list, Gianna, and no, you're right, I haven't been in touch. My work takes me away, and this makes me bad at keeping up with people—a poor excuse but that's all I've got. All I can do is to offer you my sincere condolences. How is your father?"

Her calm response was again not what he expected. "He is a complete bastard and in my eyes will always be so. Please do not ask why."

Charles felt himself reeling with the shock of this exchange; he had to compose himself. "Fine, I won't. What about your little sister?" He cursed himself almost as soon as the words were out. Using the word *piccola* made it sound like he was talking about a three-year-old child, whereas he already knew that she was a teenager. She picked up on this straightaway.

"Luisa is not a little girl any more, but a fine young woman, and I am intensely proud of her. Like me, she has had to grow up very quickly indeed. Everything she does, she does well. She is absolutely stunning, and even at the age of fourteen, it is difficult for her to fight off the attention of the boys."

"No surprise there, Gianna; in that respect I must say that you are identical." He wanted to take the initiative in this conversation and not allow her time to reply to the compliment, which he was sure she would deflect in some way. "Now, will you both please come to my hotel for dinner tonight or tomorrow night, if tonight is not enough notice for you? It will be entirely my pleasure to entertain you both. Please say yes." He realised that to have invited her father as well would have led to a total rebuff.

"Well, not tonight. I will ask my sister if she wants to come tomorrow. If she doesn't, then I won't come either.

If you contact me early tomorrow, here at the Galleria, then I will let you know. Thank you for the invitation, Mr. Court."

"It's Charles, please get used to calling me that, or Carlo if that sits easier with you." At last, a hint of a smile.

"Yes." But that was all she said apart from, "*Ci vediamo.*"

Charles played the exchange of words over and over again in his mind, analysing how well he had done this time. After the terrible beginning, he judged that he had done better than he expected. With this girl, you had to watch carefully what you said and how you phrased it. The next morning, he arrived early at the Galleria, very keen to know the response to his invitation. He prepared himself for rejection.

"Luisa says that she would like to come and meet you, and we are both looking forward to a nice evening. Can we make it at about seven? I don't like this custom we have in Italy of a late start to the meal. I get past wanting it. Luisa is the same."

"Seven it is, then. Come as early as you like. I will tell the front of house to expect you."

"Is it still the Gritti you stay at, or will you be somewhere else?"

"Always the Gritti, Gianna." He winked as he replied and she could not yet make out whether this man had style or if he just liked to show off. He got up to leave, and suddenly there was a spring in his step.

CHAPTER 7

CHANGE

"*Buonasera, Luisa. Mi chiamo Carlo …*" I did not speak any English at this stage, so it was good that Carlo spoke more than acceptable Italian with good, accurate grammar. He continued, "I know nothing about you apart from what your sister has briefly told me. It must have been very difficult for you and Gianna these past years, coping with the decline of your mother." He paused briefly. "Please don't talk about it if it upsets you but I want you to know that I understand. I too lost my mother four years ago—that's not as young as you and Gianna but I cried for a long time, I can tell you. In time you will come to terms with it, but it is a slow process."

I replied with the confidence instilled in me by my sister. She told me not to be overawed by the English Mr. Court. "We didn't cry when Mamma died, did we, Gianna? We expected it, and Gianna prepared me for it; so it wasn't so difficult. Papa, however, was in a terrible state."

Gianna reached out and touched my wrist without leaning toward me. "That's right, Luisa. Carlo, can we talk about something else please? Thank you for your concern but life has to go on, and we are here to enjoy ourselves."

"Yes, of course. Is Luisa allowed a cocktail?"

"Luisa makes her own decisions about such matters, Carlo." This made me feel very grown up but having seen what alcohol did to my father, I said I would have a fruit juice, orange would be nice. This did not stop Gianna, who had a Champagne cocktail along with Carlo. She was bold enough to ask for real French Champagne, not the local prosecco. Carlo seemed pleased by this. The drinks arrived, and she now seemed relaxed. I was pleased that she looked as if she was starting to enjoy herself.

It was a remarkably pleasant evening, and I noticed Carlo commanded great respect from the hotel staff. I had never experienced hotel service before—it was just wonderful, so nothing now can live up to what it was like that first night. This was how the super-rich lived, and Gianna, judging by her behaviour later, obviously gained a taste for it in those first meetings with Carlo. We had different wines with every course, and I tried a mouthful of each. Carlo went to great lengths to explain what they were but I can't remember what he said. It was a bit wasted on me, I'm afraid to say. I nodded at his explanations.

They began to see one another on a regular basis. Carlo took Gianna on a vacation, visiting Florence, Rome, Monte Carlo, and Paris, showing her a style of living that she previously had no idea existed, other than what she had read in books. In return, she introduced Carlo to Papa, who was polite to the point of servility, possibly because he had a fair idea of just how rich Carlo was. In the middle of June, in line with what one could only describe as a whirlwind romance, Carlo asked Papa's permission to marry Gianna, and he instantly agreed. I guess that Papa felt an enormous sense of gratitude toward Carlo because, with his views about gays, this man would have the ability to cure her finally of this "girl thing" that he so detested.

It was true Gianna was totally altered as an individual, but it was not her sexuality that had changed at all. I know this because she still went out with Alessandra and stayed at her apartment at times. Perhaps it was the many grinding years of caring for a sick mother with no support from Papa and having to be my guardian angel as well. I wonder now how much did she really love Carlo—I don't think I will ever know the answer to that question, but I rather expect that she did not love him all that much. I cannot condemn her for doing what she did, but I felt abandoned when Carlo became the focus of her life. The blow was softened to a certain extent because Carlo showed great kindness toward me, knowing that the bond between us, as sisters, was very strong indeed.

At the Galleria, they were shocked to say the least when she announced that she was leaving to get married to the Englishman Carlo Court. The director was effusive in his congratulations, but Gianna reckoned that it hid his real feelings, which were of deep disapproval. This didn't stop him from accepting the wedding invitation. It was a lavish affair but there were relatively few guests. Carlo brought his brother over from England, but I can't remember him saying anything to me. He sat with my Papa part of the time, and I saw Carlo doing his best to act as an interpreter for a short while. Other than that, he gave the impression of being socially inept and retarded, which I later found out was quite an accurate impression to have gained.

All of Gianna's girlfriends were invited, and in the evening, it was a stunning array of feminine youth and beauty that lined up inside the Gritti Palace to wish my sister and her husband well. Papa was a bit of an embarrassment because he drank too much and was very garrulous. He stayed well away from grandmother and her husband. My aunt and uncle left quite early with the excuse of having difficult journeys ahead of them. They looked uncomfortable and out of their depth. Papa, from what I could see, did not manage to communicate with them either.

He tried talking to a group of girls, and whilst telling a joke, he managed to knock over a bottle of Champagne by using wide and expansive hand gestures in the telling of his unfunny story. Later, I heard him making some drunken, suggestive comments to the girls, none of whom was in the slightest interested in him. This is not so surprising, given his age and coarse manners and also the sexual orientation of the majority of them. I can remember apologising to some of the girls for his crudity, and my politeness obviously impressed one or two of them. I could now recognise when I was being eyed up and stared at, because two of the girls paid special attention to me, which I found quite embarrassing and didn't know how to deflect. My sister, the beautiful new bride, came over and rescued me from their advances. The reception would have been a nightmare for any red-blooded heterosexual male, who would have surely drawn a blank on such an evening as this.

Gianna did not want to live in Venice; she wanted to move to London, even though Carlo did give her the choice. This was totally her decision, and the Galleria was very sad to lose her. She wanted to escape the city of her youth and all of the bad memories that went with it. When she left, she took me on one side and said something to me that I failed to fully comprehend at the time. They were words to the effect that I was never, ever to let Papa touch me in any intimate way. The reason for this, she explained, was that he had become a bit odd since Mamma had died, especially when he had a lot to drink. I took Gianna at her word, also remembering his recent behaviour at the wedding reception. What she also did not know was that I had a private viewing of all those horrible photographs before they were thrown away. She said that if he did touch me, I was to let her know at once. I solemnly agreed that she would be the first to know. She also told me not to do it with any boys until I was absolutely ready. It was advice that I readily listened to and followed.

What I was not aware of was the conversation she had held with Papa at the same time. I was to find out that she threatened him with death if she found out that he had ever tried to do to me what he had done to her. She also told him to save his energy looking for his magazines and pictures because they had been discovered and thrown away. She became furious with him when he suggested that it was Mamma who made him buy them. The woman was dead and yet he was trying to blame her for his perverted tastes. He merely shrugged and said that he could not help it if she didn't believe him. The dates on the magazines revealed that he was still buying them long after sexual relations would have ceased between him and Mamma.

It must have been a strange time for Papa because whilst he was treated with complete and utter contempt by Gianna, Carlo showered him with kindness, offering to buy him a new home in Venice away from Cannaregio. That must have made it clear to Papa that Carlo did not know what he had done to Gianna; otherwise, he would surely not have been so generous. Papa did not accept the offer of a new home but was persuaded instead to allow Carlo to pay for the apartment to be completely refurbished and redecorated. I enjoyed that but it was no substitute for losing the company of my sister. I missed her terribly. When she left Venice as a married woman, she was nineteen years old but I was still only fourteen. I buried myself in my schoolwork because I knew that was what Gianna wanted me to do. I was still completely under her spell.

It was a characteristic of almost every man in those days that he wanted the girl he was about to marry to be a virgin. It seemed that it was acceptable for a man to go off and have sex with as many women as he liked but a girl was not a nice girl unless she saved herself exclusively for the man she was going to marry. This is, of course, complete hypocrisy, but it is still a problem that Gianna faced when getting married to Carlo. In forthright style, she told him before he proposed marriage that she was not a virgin. He tried not to look disappointed, and he asked who she had been in love with. Of course, she wanted to conceal the fact that it was her own father who had caused this, so she improvised and said she had loved no one but was raped by three boys at school. Carlo was stunned by this revelation, and before he asked the inevitable questions that she did not want to answer, she spoke just as he was opening his mouth.

"You can ask my father if you want to; he will confirm it."

Carlo was full of sadness for her. "That must have been terrible for you—what happened to your attackers? Did they get away with it?"

Gianna did not want to go into too much detail but after the opening lie, it would be better to continue with the stark truth. "No Carlo; as it happens, they are all dead."

Carlo was astounded and almost dropped the glass he was holding. "Dead? All of them? Was it a bus accident or something like that?"

"No, they all separately died in mysterious circumstances in a period spanning about six weeks."

"They were murdered—is that what you are saying?"

Gianna looked him straight in the eye and, with a hint of drama, emphasised what she thought might be a stereotypical opinion that outsiders have of her country.

"Although Venice does not generally have this sort of problem, you have to remember that this is Italy, Carlo."

"Did your father," he hesitated, "you know, have anything to do with it?" He felt that this was a reasonable question, although it risked offending her. Judging by the response he got, it appeared not to.

"He was away on business every time the murders happened and was cleared by the polizia because all of his alibis checked out. His theory is that other families with young daughters must have taken revenge. Why don't you speak to Papa about it? He will tell you exactly what happened. For me, it is still too painful to talk about. But I don't regret what happened to them after what they did to me."

"Of course, of course. Not another word, I promise you."

These truths mixed up with lies were enough to convince Carlo that his intended future partner was telling him the whole truth and that there was no need to check the story out. Well, not immediately, he didn't. Using his connections, he did decide to make enquiries and he discovered that three murders of Venice teenagers had taken place in 1962 as she described. He felt ashamed of himself for not having fully believed her, and one day shortly after, he apologised to her for giving the impression that he had ever doubted her word.

This apology was graciously accepted by Gianna, who inwardly heaved a sigh of relief.

CHAPTER 8

SWINGING LONDON

Gianna found herself in London at the end of an era and, by definition, the start of a new one. It was late summer 1964 when she arrived, and within a few weeks the country had elected a new government. It was thought it would take more than this one election to break the dominance of the last thirteen years of Conservative rule, particularly in the rural shires, but Harold Wilson, the Labour leader, swept to power on a tide of optimism (but with only a narrow majority in the House of Commons). Gianna was to learn that it was a major social change that brought about the end of the Conservatives being in power. She wanted to know what was going on in her newly adopted country; Carlo took the trouble to explain what was happening so that she didn't feel so isolated. In addition to having the *Times* delivered every day, which she was able to pick up and read, he subscribed to the satirical magazine *Private Eye*. According to him, it printed the news and stories that the daily papers would not dare to publish. When it was published each fortnight, he would tell her the meaning of the front cover, which as it still does today had irreverent captions in balloons coming out of the mouths of pictured politicians, members of the royal family, or other celebrities of the day.

A sex scandal had played a fair part in the form of the Profumo affair that, in the end, saw the patrician Harold Macmillan stand down from office in October 1963. It was rumoured that amongst the ruling classes and aristocracy, there were parties and orgies taking place with the hiring in of girls to entertain the participants. Mixed up in all this, John Profumo was a government minister who was partial to call girls who were also involved with attachés to the Soviet Embassy, who may well have been spies. This took place at a time when the cold war was at its height, following the building of the Berlin Wall and the Cuban missile crisis. It provoked mass hysteria and outrage at what seemed like an establishment cover-up. Quite apart from this, Macmillan was by now in poor health, and by this time, the sun had well and truly set upon the British Empire, as one by one the colonies had gained full independence from the mother country.

The dull 1950s had given way to the 1960s, and there was a new mood amongst young people, with a revolution in the pop music scene led by bands from Merseyside, the most prominent of which were the Beatles. More important than this was the rise of the working man, backed up by a Trade Union movement that was gathering strength and momentum. For the first time since the end of the Second World War, this class of people had real disposable income and the aspirations to go with it. This was not just in London but all over the United Kingdom.

The Conservatives, in office for the past thirteen years, looked stuffy and old-fashioned, still dominated by the landed gentry and supported financially in the main by the privileged upper classes. It was no wonder they lost the election with a leader like Sir Alec Douglas Home replacing Macmillan. Home was portrayed as a grouse-shooting aristocrat, totally out of touch with ordinary people. He only had one year to turn the tide after Macmillan stood down, and he was not helped by being mercilessly ridiculed in *Private Eye*. The pipe-smoking, avuncular Wilson, who had become Labour leader in early 1963, was the man of the moment and seemingly a man of the people. However, it wasn't all that long after he was elected before he, along with his sidekick George Brown, was also being lampooned in *Private Eye*. Brown at times did not help his own cause by coming across as pompous and also having a penchant for drink.

I remember Gianna describing her new social circle, which contained many Champagne Socialists (like her husband), and it seemed to be fashionable to call yourself a Socialist even if outward appearances said otherwise. In this new circle, you were either "with it" or you were a "square." It was bad news if you were considered a square but it was worse if you pretended to be with it and it was later discovered that your attitudes meant that you were really a square. There is something rather pathetic when you see an older man trying to act as if he is young. Gianna said there were plenty of people like that who pretended that they appreciated the new wave of pop music whilst in private they detested it. Some also thought it was a good idea to grow their hair long, which only made them look ridiculous.

As a young, beautiful woman wearing all the latest Carnaby Street fashions and living in London, Gianna would have most certainly been with it because she could carry it off so effortlessly. As a result, Charles would have been looked upon in the same way, especially as she called him Carlo. Her life seemed to be an endless round of parties, and because Charles had connections in the art world, she came into contact with many celebrities, pop stars, and wealthy people. Gianna was never required in her new life to get a job independently of Carlo, and it never occurred to her to follow any kind of career. She was enjoying herself far too much to resort to this mundane type of existence. It was a frivolous lifestyle but one she was prepared to fully embrace. It was I think a huge reaction to what she had been through in her early teenage years. As she could converse fluently in three different languages and could also get by well in French, she was a popular guest at all the cosmopolitan parties to which they were invited, and she did Charles a power of good when he was exhibiting work by engaging with customers from most European countries as well as the United States of America.

If guests and prospective customers did not speak English, then German or French was likely to at least be their second language, and with the Italian visitors she was always an instant hit. The UK has always had this reputation for lagging about ten years behind the United States in business terms but Carlo, who had been to America several times, adapted his business to the techniques he had seen used there. He was really switched on when it came to selling. He did it by using Gianna as a public relations person to front the gallery, and she exuded magnetism based on her sexuality and knew how to use it. This was an early example of the marketing revolution in the United Kingdom and the realisation that sex can help you to sell almost anything. Charles reckoned that he sold many pieces of work because of Gianna, even though she did not profess to know very much about art despite her experience back in Venice at the Galleria. He said it didn't matter but her presence there at the exhibitions did. It also helped that he had a bevy of beauties there handing out cocktails, turning the viewings into parties. He hosted events that everyone wanted to attend.

It was all very exciting to begin with, but eventually Gianna grew bored of these events, even though it did allow her to meet some new and interesting people. But associated with the interesting ones were quite a few who were very tiresome indeed. In the end, it must be said that boredom was a factor that led to her eventual downfall.

Gianna, married to Carlo, became part of the Mayfair set. This high life included lavish parties, casino gambling, West End nightclubs, and the recreational use of drugs like cocaine and LSD. The final component in this new decadent lifestyle was, of course, sexual promiscuity. Gianna was quite prepared to be the dutiful wife in the bedroom, but her new life brought her into contact with some women who were bisexual or gay like herself. Most of these women had marriages of convenience, and others were actually straight but liked to experiment. As a younger woman, she found herself a target rather than a predator, and this suited her fine. This was how it had been when she had her first experiences of this kind at school. She also found herself pursued by men and at times bothered by unwanted telephone calls and even stalked.

One evening, a female admirer told her that she was a trophy wife, something that had to be explained to her. She was quite certain that Carlo was having affairs with other women whilst on his travels, but this did not bother her unduly. He was very often away, and this gave her the freedom to do what she wanted. She wasn't very interested in the men who pursued her but agreed to dispense her favours in exchange for large sums of money. If anybody was infatuated enough to present her with gifts, as often happened, then these would be sold and the proceeds stored away. Gianna had turned herself into a highly paid paramour, not unlike an eighteenth-century Venetian courtesan plying her trade up and down the Grand Canal. I don't know whether she would have liked this comparison, but I rather think she wouldn't have cared.

In the sixties, despite the sexual revolution, there was still no general acceptance of gays (homosexuals, as they were routinely called in those days). Men could still be prosecuted until the mid-sixties, and homosexuality, which had been an offence since 1885, was not decriminalised until July 1967. Before then, it was looked upon by most reactionaries and even lots of ordinary people as an illness or a perverted life choice. The attitude of the law toward gay women was less clear, and it was beyond the imaginations of many that women did that kind of thing. Thank goodness we live in more enlightened times, even though there are still lots of Neanderthals around who still hold those antiquated views. Even when the law changed, being gay was still something you didn't shout proudly about from the rooftops because of the social stigma attached to it. This, of course, is not like today when at times it is the complete opposite.

Gianna found that the summer season of social events took her to Ascot, where she loved the dressing up; to Henley to watch the rowing, which she didn't like because of the boorish type of people she encountered; to Wimbledon, which she enjoyed; and to Lord's, where she didn't understand what was going on despite the attempts of a few ardent admirers to explain the intricacies of cricket. Each of these events would end with a party somewhere. Did these people drink anything other than Champagne? It seemed not.

It turned out that Charles loved the thrill of gambling and knew where all the illegal clubs were. He also liked to organise gambling sessions himself. One night, this led to a nasty incident. One member of their social circle was Cecil Smith, a former high-ranking army officer who had a good war, as they liked to say. His daughter Hayley was having an on/off affair with Gianna, and he found out about it when he caught them in bed together. His reaction was not to remonstrate with his daughter but to try and blackmail Gianna into sleeping with him, but this did not work. Gianna was revolted just by the very physical appearance of Cecil Smith and was not intimidated at all. "I am sure that Hayley will be pleased when you tell all of Mayfair and everyone knows that she is infatuated with me," Gianna said. "I know that Carlo will find out but I will explain that your daughter is pursuing me and won't leave me alone. So go ahead, I don't care."

Cecil realised that blackmail wasn't going to work, so he tried something else. "I've heard that you're the type that will do it for money. Is that true?" He sneered when he said this, still hoping that the answer would be in the affirmative.

"That isn't true," lied Gianna in reply, "but even if it were true, then my answer would be still be no, not with you. Not ever."

One evening after a heavy drinking session at Raymond's Revue Bar in Soho, a dozen of the circle went back to Miles Wilson's large mews house in Pimlico to play "Escalado." This is a horse racing game, where five horses are placed on a piece of lightweight canvas secured to a table. The canvas, which is rolled out from a control box with a winding mechanism, is stretched tight and then through winding the box, the vibration moves the horses forward. The die-cast metal horses can hit obstacles (fences) and lose ground or even fall over. The outcome of the races is never sure, as misfortune can befall the leading horse on the brink of victory. Carlo organised four teams of three that would bet large sums on the outcome. Each syndicate would draw a horse colour: red, yellow, blue, green, or white.

If the undrawn horse won any race, the money would carry over into the next round. The stakes could get quite high, increasing usually with the level of drunken excitement. There is no skill in this table-top game— it is a game of chance and almost impossible to cheat. Gianna was, on this occasion, in a syndicate with Miles and a rather effete-looking homosexual named Richard Ashton, who had made his fortune from publishing. The atmosphere on such evenings was very competitive and usually friendly, but this time, unsuitable comments started quite early on in the proceedings from the mouth of Cecil Smith. In an early round, his horse hit one of the fences and rebounded and looked for a moment that it was going backwards. "Look, it's going backwards," he crowed in dismay, "just like an Italian tank. You know all about Italian tanks, don't you—one forward gear and three reverse for a quick retreat. Haw, haw, haw!"

Surprisingly, it was the normally passive Ashton who spoke first. "That is an old joke, Cecil, and not very funny, especially in present company. And another thing, my father fought in the Western Desert during the war, and he said that the Italians that he fought against were a formidable enemy and definitely not as you like to portray them with your witless jokes."

The room went suddenly quiet, with the impervious Cecil replying defensively but still laughing at his own witticism. "All right, steady on, no hard feelings, only having a bit of fun!"

Then why say it? thought Gianna, who had heard the joke quite a few times before. She was never one to dress herself up in her national flag but the remarks made about her country seemed childish. She nodded with appreciation toward Ashton, and he briefly smiled back at her. However, no matter, they got on with the game, and her syndicate drew the blue horse. All was going well in this round as the toy horses set off. The stakes were high because it was late in the evening and the previous two rounds had been won, quite unusually, by the undrawn colour. The carryover pot of money was in the region of a thousand pounds, the equivalent of a year's salary for many working class people. So, that was a great deal of money in those days. The blue horse was still clear but struck the last obstacle and fell sideways, bringing down the yellow and green. The red horse, backed by the syndicate led by Cecil Smith, came through from a poor fourth position to win the pot of money, and the victory was greeted by huge and noisy celebrations. The cheering died down finally, and Cecil wanted to rub his good fortune in and to needle Gianna, who had a couple of days ago rejected his sexual advances with devastating finality.

"Never mind, Gianna, you can always join our syndicate—you know, change sides like you did in the war!"

Miles Wilson didn't mind losing the race but, as a secret admirer of Gianna, didn't like the remark at all, noticing that Ashton had also coloured up with anger. His English cut-glass accent sounded clearly above the noise in the room.

"That's bloody offensive, Cecil—apologise at once; Gianna had nothing to do with the war you keep going on about."

Cecil, full of alcohol as well as jubilation at his victory, blustered, "Not bloody likely, I fought against her lot in the desert, and a rotten lot they were too!" Miles, angry and face now deep red, strode forward and punched Cecil full in the face, and he fell to the floor; he sat up clutching his bleeding nose and cried out, "You bastard, you've broken my nose—I'll sue you."

"And the whole room full of people will say you tripped over in a drunken state and did it to yourself. Now get out of my house, Cecil, and don't even think about coming anywhere near me until you have learned some manners and make a full written apology to Gianna and Charles!" By this time, Miles had hold of him and was pushing him out of the door with his foot, aiming kicks up his backside. "Go on," he commanded, "out!" Miles returned, his face still flushed, to the room full of guests who were murmuring amongst themselves.

"My dear Gianna, I am so sorry. Some people just cannot forget the war, I'm afraid. And Charles, dear boy, words fail me—Cecil Smith is a buffoon."

Gianna shrugged her shoulders. "When I see him next, perhaps I will have to tell him the stories of my mother's experiences in the resistance as a young girl in Venice. She risked her life as well." The room fell silent; not even Carlo knew this. The fun had well and truly gone out of the party, and it was time to go home. Carlo called up a taxi, and within a few minutes, it arrived and they settled into the back seat for the short journey home.

"I am really sorry that I never met your mother. She must have been a remarkable woman. Do you know what she did during the war exactly?"

"From what I could gather, she mainly ran messages and took food, guns, and other packages to safe houses. This was often done right under the noses of the German soldiers, with whom she used to flirt. They never suspected her at all, but if they had found out, she would have been shot."

"What did your father think of this?"

"It is something that is never discussed with him because she met and fell in love with a young resistance fighter. She thought my father had been killed, as there had been no word from him for over a year. It is one of those things that happen in war."

"My goodness—everyone has his own story about the war, but a pig-headed boor like Cecil Smith is too thick to see it other than through his own eyes."

"He should know better." Both of them now lapsed into silence as the taxi took them home.

I try to imagine what it was like to be caught up in this type of life, which was all part of swinging London in the mid-1960s. If her diaries were at all a representative portrayal of life then, it did not make me envious of not having been a part of it.

CHAPTER 9

MY SISTER: THE COURTESAN

I knew about the insult that Gianna had received from Cecil Smith at the party because she told me over the telephone, but only her diary told me of the aftermath. Gianna answered the door to her Mayfair apartment the following morning, still in her dressing gown, even though it was not far short of midday. It was a familiar face that was there on the threshold, and she invited him in. Miles was still full of apologies for what happened the previous night. What, she wondered, prompted Miles to call around and see them? Charles was not there, and she remembered him telling Miles that he would be away from early Sunday. Gianna also wondered whether it was a peculiarly British thing to apologise for something that you had not done. However, she was ready to frankly explain what had sparked off the incident and tell Miles whether he wanted to hear it or not.

"He thinks I am a bad influence over his daughter, despite the fact that she is two years older than me. It is pathetic, isn't it? Surely, you would think, she knows her own mind by now and doesn't need him to stand over her telling her what she can and can't do."

Miles was intrigued by what she had said and asked, "In what way a bad influence?"

"She has a crush on me. Is that the right expression in English? We had some fun together and he found out. So he knows this and thinks that I should sleep with him and then he would agree to keep the whole thing quiet."

"I think I understand," said Miles, whose mind was racing, "and I'm sorry, it is really none of my business."

Gianna was making coffee, and Miles was alone for a minute with his own thoughts. Hayley Smith seemed to develop a crush on many people she came into contact with and wasn't too fussy who she slept with, as he had found out for himself. She was the kind of girl who got passed around from one person to the next. Quite good in bed, he seemed to recall, but a bit of a screamer and moaner who liked it a bit rough. She tried to turn men on by putting on a baby voice and acting as if butter wouldn't melt in her mouth. What was it she said one night before he had her, "Do you want me to dress up for you like a naughty schoolgirl, Milesey-Wilesey?" If Cecil Smith knew the full extent of his daughter's behaviour, then he would be even more upset. It would earn Miles a punch in the face in return for having slept with her. He was glad that Gianna didn't feel it necessary to go to bed with that buffoon Cecil Smith. She interrupted his thoughts, which had already run away with him. He noticed that thinking about all of this had got him aroused, and he would now have to fight to control the erection that had been triggered. She was speaking again, and he tried to concentrate.

"You really didn't have to hit him like that, Miles. I don't need my honour to be defended, and I am wondering why you reacted in that manner. I don't mean to be as offensive as Cecil but I have caught you staring at me many times; I guess you would like to sleep with me even though you are probably Carlo's best friend."

"Gianna, I'm embarrassed—I think I had better leave." Miles, reeling under the directness of these comments, realised that he had been found out.

"But it's true, isn't it?" She sensed his discomfort and pressed on just the same. "Tell me, Miles, do you know if Carlo has other women? You are his friend, you can tell me—it doesn't make any difference to me. After all, I am no saint, as you have just discovered."

"I don't know what to say. I think Charles is able to exercise a certain amount of power over the opposite sex. He had girlfriends before he met you, but I don't know of anything going on at the moment, not that he would boast about it or tell me for that matter. I think he has charisma and is a natural charmer."

Gianna interrupted. "Charisma. That's a good word. He's not much good in the bedroom, I can tell you that. Especially for a man who is supposed to be as experienced as you say."

"Gianna, for goodness sake, please stop!" But before he could protest any more, Gianna was goading him, moving a couple of paces in his direction. He was now fully aroused, and it showed. It was clear that Gianna had noticed it also.

"Sex—is that all you want, Miles? You can get that anywhere around here. You have to pay for it, of course. You won't get it from me either; well, not for free. Is that what you're looking for?" She pulled at his tie. "You knew that Carlo would not be here this morning—I heard him tell you."

"I am doing this out of friendship, and I am here because I am concerned!" He was blustering and knew that he didn't sound very convincing.

"Friendship? The trouble with friendship is that some people can't do it without the sex, can they? I tell you what, Miles, when Carlo is next away, you can take me out to dinner and we'll see how we get along—unless you want to stay for a while now and show me how concerned you are."

Gianna moved further toward him, and the front of her dressing gown came open, revealing that she was completely naked underneath, and Miles, being Miles, could not resist. This had taken him completely by surprise, even though it was something he had wanted to do for some considerable time. She made him use a contraceptive, a packet of which he always carried with him. He didn't like putting one on, but for him it was still an enjoyable fifteen minutes as he thrust himself deep inside her, letting out an extraordinary noise when he reached his climax. If she was faking it (her diary indicates that she was), then she was damned good at it. The real problem for him now was that he had to conceal his obsession for Gianna from Charles. Once Miles had slept with Gianna, he now detested the fact that Gianna did not reserve her favours just for him alone. He would throw money at the problem, hoping that it would keep her faithful to him. Gianna kept the money and carried on behaving the same as before. He could tolerate her being with other women, because privately he was fascinated by what he imagined lesbians got up to. But when it came to other men, it would drive him mad with jealousy to think she was having sex with them.

Even at this early stage of their affair, Miles started to stalk Gianna. Eventually, she realised what he was doing and reflected that he probably had been for some time. On first discovery, she thought it was quite funny. One evening she was in Snow's, a dive bar just off Piccadilly Circus, in the company of Andrea Hannington, one of her bisexual girlfriends. Miles had followed her surreptitiously into this establishment and had taken a seat over the far side of the bar, where he didn't think he would be seen. He was pretending to read the evening newspaper. Gianna knew he was there and asked Andrea to give her a hug and then a lingering kiss full on.

"What! In front of everyone here? You'll get us thrown out!" Andrea exclaimed, full of excitement.

"Yes, I want to shock Miles. He's over in the corner. Sometimes he stalks me. Go on, do it—just for a laugh!" Andrea duly obliged her friend. The young man observing this from behind the bar was too embarrassed to say anything and frantically scanned the bar for customers to serve. In the background, the jukebox pumped out the sound of the Animals' number, *We Gotta Get Out of This Place*, with its deep baseline; music for the moment. The passionate kiss ended and Gianna whispered, "Now let's walk out in front of him!"

Andrea was now enjoying this piece of theatre and called over to Miles in a very loud voice, with a wave as she left arm in arm with Gianna, "Coooeee, Miles darling! We're out on the piss, do you want to join us, darling? You can protect us from any unwanted attention!"

"Er … Hello, fancy seeing you here." He looked and sounded distinctly uncomfortable. "Not tonight, ladies, I'm busy."

"Busy? Doesn't look like it, Miles!" Gianna said loudly, and by now he was feeling severely embarrassed. The two of them started off up the steps of the dive bar, leaving Miles to deal with the stares of the other customers.

Andrea stopped halfway up the stairs and looked back down into the bar before shouting, "Now Miles, you naughty boy, no looking up our skirts! Byeee." She waved, turned, wiggled her back side, and went. It was a moment when he would have liked the ground to open up and swallow him.

"He's no gentleman," a slightly drunken Andrea said excitedly as they hit the fresh air outside. "He never even stood up to speak to us."

"That was probably because he had an erection from just watching us and couldn't move without upending the table."

Andrea screamed with laughter as they hurried along Coventry Street toward Leicester Square and their next drinking destination. Gianna thought that this event might discourage Miles from stalking altogether but it did not, and she started to become agitated about it. But she did not confront him because he was a useful source of money. Miles never mentioned the incident in the dive bar, not even in passing.

Carlo stopped organising his gambling evenings after that night with Cecil Smith, who remained *persona non grata* and whose social death was created by the incident. Instead, Carlo stuck to the clubs, where the gambling was even more serious, as at times it was for very high stakes indeed. He liked to go to one or two of the clubs run by Ronnie and Reggie Kray. In those days, they were widely seen as charming and prosperous celebrity nightclub owners—all part of the swinging scene in London. It gave Carlo access to the celebrity circuit, and he and Gianna and the others were able to socialise with Lords, MPs, socialites, and show business characters. He especially liked being in the company of Diana Dors, who would treat him playfully like a little boy. She would come over to their table for drinks on occasions and ruffle his hair or sit on his lap. He loved it, and she liked to tease him. "Gianna, I'm stealing your husband. It will only be for the weekend, is that okay with you?"

"Take him away, you are welcome. It will be quite boring; he will want to show you his pictures."

"That should be okay; I'll show him mine before we're finished!"

Later on back at the apartment, Gianna decided to tease Carlo as well. "You really like Diana, don't you, Carlo?"

"Yes I do. She's really good fun. I think she's had a bit of a life, you know, but just the same, a great sense of humour."

"Why don't you bring her home and sleep with her? I think it is what you would both like to do."

"Gianna! How much have you had to drink?" But he could see that she was smiling at him.

"Just teasing!"

Another favourite haunt where they liked to go was the Astor Club. Toward the end of the year, the Astor would have a Christmas party. It was here that a gangster turf war started. At the same party were the Richardson brothers and a very loud-mouthed member of their criminal gang named George Cornell, who during the course of the evening got progressively drunk and called Ronnie Kray a fat poof, a reference to his well-known sexual proclivities. It was done as loudly as possible to try and cause Ronnie the maximum amount of discomfort. This caused a massive brawl and the party broke up. Gianna had stumbled upon this nasty side of living in the capital and began to hear about the gruesome methods used by the Richardson brothers, and their gang members. They were still discussing it two days later.

"Carlo, this is the Mafia, only London style. Some of these people would fit in very well in Sicily or Napoli. I am told that they torture people who don't do as they say. Perhaps we should stay away from these clubs from now on."

"The problem with that suggestion, Gianna, is that I have done business with some people over the years who are associated directly with them. You will always find that bad men get connected with wealthy people—that is how they make their money, either honestly or more than likely dishonestly. Sometimes, the celebrities you see get themselves heavily into debt at the tables. This gives the Kray boys a hold over them. They owe 'the house' money but they are not asked to pay it just as long as they keep turning up and bringing their friends and showing their faces. Even if they have not got a hold over you in this way, it is also an inescapable fact that sometimes they can be useful if you want a job done."

"That sounds illegal."

"You're learning, Gianna. Sometimes it is illegal. But that is the way it is."

"Are you saying that Ronnie and Reggie are also bad people?"

"Well, they are East End of London boys who have made good. Both of them have done time in prison, but there again, so has my own brother so I don't sit in judgment on them—and nor should you." He gave her a bit of a lecture on people only being a product of the environment in which they grew up and that some fall into crime quite easily. Gianna's mind went back to the activities of her father and how the three boys who had tried to rape her had been dealt with. Inwardly she shuddered as she tried to focus on the points that Carlo was making.

"The boys do very well but the trouble starts when someone wants a piece of what you've got. Just watch them turn nasty if anyone tries to muscle in on their territory. I know they sail quite close to the wind at times but they seem to know all the right people, and by that I mean some senior officers in Scotland Yard, you know, the police." He qualified this just in case she did not understand fully what he was saying. He finished off his observations by saying, "They have found that police officers can be bribed as well as anyone else. The danger for those two is if they start to think they are untouchable. I am friendly with them but like to keep them somewhat at arm's length."

"Do you owe them money?"

"No, I don't. When I gamble, I know when to stop."

"They are always so nice to me, and they seem to like us, but what you're saying is 'don't cross them'?"

"Exactly, don't get on the wrong side of the Kray boys. I have a feeling there is going to be more trouble but let's hope not. I don't think Richardson and his friends will ever be allowed back in the Astor after what happened the other night."

CHAPTER 10

1966

Nothing stays the same forever. My dear husband often reminds me of this. The start of the New Year was insignificant, but as winter turned into spring, it brought about a number of incidents that made a remarkable impact at the time. And one event had repercussions over forty years later, but first things first.

The turf war between the Krays and Richardsons continued. On the seventh of March, a man named Richard Hart was shot in another brawl, this time at Mr. Smith's Club in Bushey Green, Catford, in southeast London. Mr. Hart was a direct associate of the Krays and one of their enforcers cum negotiators. Both gangs believed they had the protection rights over this club, which was owned by Manchester-based businessmen Flood and Benny. The disagreement turned into a verbal slanging match and then a fistfight and then a shoot-out, with a number of people ending up in hospital. One of the Richardsons gang by the name of Jimmy Andrews went for treatment the day after the fray to Whitechapel Hospital.

George Cornell, who had started the bust-up in the Astor Club, went to visit his friend Jimmy and, on exiting the hospital, was seen walking down the Whitechapel Road like a man possessed—swearing his head off, either drunk or on drugs, possibly both. He burst into the Blind Beggar pub at about 8:30 PM and started to shout insults about the Krays, knowing that this was a place that the boys frequented.

"Where's that fat wanker?" he shouted to all and sundry.

Witnessing all of this was Carlo, who was due to meet Ronnie to discuss a painting that an associate of his wanted to get hold of. He wanted Carlo to do the bidding at the auction because he knew how it worked. Kray was late, which for him was unusual. It turned out that he was drinking in another pub nearby and received a call from the Blind Beggar that he was being bad-mouthed by Cornell in the saloon bar.

Carlo had already recognised Cornell from the Astor and could see that his behaviour was upsetting people, and it was getting nasty. With Kray not there yet, he decided to leave and was already near the door and about to go when he saw Ronnie arrive through the saloon bar door with two other associates he didn't recognise. He heard Cornell, who by now was very drunk indeed, call out, "Well, look what the dog's brought in." It turned out to be his final words.

Ronnie didn't see Carlo as he entered the saloon, as he was obviously intent on Cornell, whom he approached and shot in the head with his gun at close range as he sat at the bar. A very frightened Carlo decided that it was time he was gone and would later tell Ronnie that he saw nothing because he was in the toilet and went home when he heard the shots ring out.

Carlo told Gianna what had happened but made her swear never to tell anyone else. He said the safest thing to do was to carry on as if nothing had happened. Carlo was sure that the killing was linked to what had happened in Catford two nights before and seemed to be very shaken up about it. Gianna reflected that all Carlo had previously said about these people was correct and stored the story away for another day. Due to intimidation, no witnesses ever came forward to cooperate with the police on the Blind Beggar shooting. Gianna was not surprised because she certainly knew all about keeping silent at the right time.

The next incident in that year came about as a direct result of Gianna's continued dalliance with Miles. How do you keep an illicit affair secret? Answer—reduce the chances of anyone finding out by meeting up on neutral territory where you are not likely to be seen. Miles devised these elaborate trysts and made Gianna get the train from Victoria Mainline Station out to West Dulwich a few miles up the line toward Crystal Palace. He would drive out to the small suburban station and pick her up. They would go to a local hotel half a mile away in Thurlow Hill and have sex. Afterwards, they would invariably go to a public house in Dulwich Village, called the Crown and Greyhound, which had become very fashionable. It had developed a good restaurant with a decent wine cellar to match, which was quite unusual in those days. Toward the end of the week from Thursdays through to Sundays, it was usually crowded, especially after nine o'clock in the evening. This was the time that the pair of them generally left to make their way back up to the centre of town after they had taken dinner.

They would go roughly every other week. Gianna would tell Carlo that she reserved Thursday night for meeting up with girlfriends, and of course, every other week she did. She could always rely on Andrea Hannington to cover for her, and she did the same for her. Andrea was not yet thirty and married to a wealthy stockbroker in the City of London who, like Carlo, was never home. She had developed a voracious appetite for younger men, who she managed to pick up from one of these newly setup escort agencies sited in the West End of London.

You could say that Gianna and Andrea were bad for one another but it was an arrangement that worked for both of them.

On one Thursday evening, service in the "Dog," as the Crown and Greyhound was known, was for some unknown reason unaccountably slow, so they did not leave until just before ten o'clock. It was the week after the Blind Beggar shooting. Miles as usual had been drinking his fair quota of wine, finishing off with a double brandy. As they were late, he was in a hurry to get back up to town.

The date was 17 March 1966, and the British Prime Minister, Harold Wilson, had recently called a General Election to be held on 31 March. Labour no longer had a working majority in the House of Commons from the 1964 election victory because of bye-election defeats, and Wilson was returning to the country for a fresh mandate. The respective parties were out canvassing, and after a cold and dispiriting night on the doorsteps of the Dulwich Parliamentary constituency, a group of local Young Conservatives were just arriving at the pub for a couple of post-canvassing drinks. This was just as Miles and Gianna were leaving to get back up to Central London.

The general consensus amongst these young supporters was that their party was in for a heavy beating. The canvass returns were poor, and in the marginal wards there were more houses with yellow and red posters in their windows, bearing the name of Labour's Sam Silkin, than there were blue ones carrying the name of the Conservative, Martin Stevens. This always, in those days, provided a rough guide as to the way the voting outcome would be.

One of the young men who had been canvassing from door to door in the cold for the Conservatives was Nigel Ricketts, and he safely swung across the road on his new Vespa Sportique motor scooter in order to park opposite the pub. He completed the manoeuvre and had positioned his vehicle at the kerb side when a car travelling at speed clipped the side of the scooter, with its front bumper knocking it over and throwing Ricketts off his bike. He was projected forward off his bike and his head came into contact with a lamp post. Ricketts had already removed his crash helmet, which exacerbated the effect of the impact to his skull. The car halted briefly about fifty metres ahead but then drove on.

Inside the car that had been driven at speed was Miles Wilson, with Gianna as his passenger. Gianna told him urgently to stop because he had hit something. He did so briefly and looked in his rear-view mirror.

"It's just a parked motorcycle—we really can't stop, we're so late."

"No, go back, Miles, it might be someone, and I can see people running across the road."

"No, no, it's okay." As Miles was in control of the vehicle, short of getting out there and then, there was not much Gianna could do but she fretted about it all the way home.

"You may have hit someone, Miles."

"I'm sure I didn't—it was the bike I clipped."

In the meantime, back outside the pub, an ambulance was now in attendance with a police car. The policeman was calling for witnesses. Two brothers who were at the side of their friend's body had seen it clearly enough and came forward. Christopher and Roger Gregson were both Young Conservatives and friends of Nigel Ricketts, who was now on a stretcher being loaded carefully into the back of the ambulance.

"We saw it happen," said Christopher, the younger of the two, to the policeman, with indignation in his voice. "The car was doing at least forty and clipped him. Then he stopped. Then he drove on."

"Did you get the number of the car, either of you?"

"No, it was too far ahead of us. It happened so fast."

"What about the colour?"

"Too dark, I'm afraid, but it was dark paint rather than light I would say. Possibly dark blue."

"Make?"

"No, but it was low to the ground and looked like some kind of sports job."

The brothers gave their details to the police and went to their home in Burbage Road, West Dulwich. There was no thought of getting a drink now. Their home was ten minutes walk from the public house, and when they got in, they persuaded their father to take them by car to Kings College Hospital on Denmark Hill, where at

1:20 AM Nigel Ricketts died of his head injuries without regaining consciousness. This incident was not witnessed but remembered very clearly by the third brother, Steve Gregson (he became my second husband all those years later), who was fourteen at the time and recalled them going to and returning from the hospital that dreadful night.

The incident made it into the newspapers, and when Gianna got on the telephone to Miles, she was furious with him. This hit-and-run crime was not going to be solved, and it played terribly on the conscience of my sister, who could not persuade Miles to own up to it. He begged her not to go to the police, and after a week of agonising over this, she agreed on one condition.

The newspapers had revealed where the two brothers who witnessed the crime lived. Gianna said her silence could be bought if Miles anonymously gave £2,000 in cash to the victim's family. She would deliver it, and her plan was that the two boys would pass it on. She figured that Miles could well afford this sum of money. She also knew the boys' surname from the newspapers and went to great lengths to find out where they lived. The best way to come by this information was to look in the voters' list kept in the public library that serves the area in which the family lived. She travelled to the main library in Southwark and asked the librarian for assistance to find Burbage Road, West Dulwich, S.E.21, and found it was listed in College Ward. It was easy then to match the house number to the family name despite the fact that it was quite a long road to research.

Two days later on 31 March, which was Election Day in Great Britain and Northern Ireland, she took a mainline train from Victoria to Herne Hill Station, which was one stop before she usually got off the train. She made her exit from the station and passed a record shop that was playing a song very loudly (it was, in her view, very appropriate that it should be the newly released Spencer Davis Group number of *Somebody Help Me*, which was soon to go to the top of the charts). "Somebody help *me*," she found herself saying softly as she tried to find the turn on to the road called Half Moon Lane, which would take her on to the correct route. She had to ask, as she was completely disoriented and already lost, having taken the wrong exit out of the station. She asked in the record shop and was sent on her way with the correct directions. She found that the house was at the opposite end from the start of the road in Herne Hill.

In total, it took her over twenty minutes to find the house, and by the time she got there, she was perspiring quite freely, something that was heavily contributed to by feelings of anxiousness. She delivered the money in cash through the letter box of the Gregson household, along with a typed note requesting the money be passed on to the bereaved family. Wearing dark glasses and a coat with the fur collar turned up, she retreated down the garden path of the neat house and back in the direction of Herne Hill and the railway station. The young Steve Gregson, who was off school with a heavy cold, heard the thud through the letter box, and as the morning post had already been delivered, he looked out of the upstairs window and saw this stranger, a woman, disappearing down the road.

As it was Election Day, he thought it was something to do with that. He watched her go out of sight and went down to find a thick envelope with all this money inside—more than he had ever seen in his life. When the family assembled that evening, he excitedly babbled the story to them, and they discussed the situation. The idea of going to the police first was debated but rejected, a decision that the local constabulary later criticised them for making. In accordance with the request, the money was given to the Ricketts family, together with note. The Ricketts family went to the police the next day with the story, and the young boy was questioned and asked for a description of the woman who had delivered the money, which didn't prove to be very helpful. The package, particularly the outer envelope, was dusted for fingerprints but the donor or donors had obviously worn gloves.

On the day itself, Gianna, now mentally exhausted, arrived home early in the evening and found Carlo already home. She now dreaded the interrogation that she was going to get regarding her whereabouts for the past few hours. This often was the case. Instead, he surprised her by saying, "Turn on the television, can you, *cara*?" Gianna suddenly remembered that it was Election Day. The early evening broadcasters were warming to the task, even though the polls had not shut yet.

"Have they given the score yet?"

"No, Carlo, you know the voting has not finished yet."

"No, not that, I mean the game." Apparently there was a football match going on somewhere. "Keep listening, can you, whilst I get you a drink? Remember, we are going to watch the election results come in at Miles's place tonight after we've been to dinner. I've booked a table at

L'ecu de France, around the corner from the gallery. After that we'll go on; it should be an interesting evening."

Gianna didn't like that particular restaurant; the last time she had been there, she had to send her steak back because it was very tough, and she felt the waiting staff were very ungracious about it. Whilst she was having these thoughts, Carlo's request was answered. The broadcaster gave the news of the game.

"And the first result we have tonight is from Hull, not the parliamentary seat but the FA Cup replay being held today, rather than this evening so that it doesn't interfere with people wanting to vote." The score came up: Hull City 1, Chelsea 3. Carlo, although a dedicated rugby man, loved Chelsea Football Club and sometimes went to home games at Stamford Bridge. Gianna detested anything to do with football and gave him the information he had been waiting for in a bored voice.

"It says Hull City 1, Chelsea 3."

A shout of triumph came from the bedroom—Carlo had forgotten the drink he was supposed to be getting for her and was now getting changed. This would, however, put him in a good mood. He came back into the room, punching the air. This was a display of adolescence that Gianna was now used to, and she ignored his celebrations.

"Now all we need is a Labour landslide, and that will make my day."

But Gianna's mind was elsewhere.

"Carlo, after dinner, can you drop me home? I don't want to watch the election." What she didn't want was to see Miles.

"Are you sure? All the gang are going to be there."

Not a good enough reason, thought Gianna, and she confirmed that she would give it a miss.

If I fast forward now to the present, two years ago to be more accurate, Miles Wilson was convicted of the murder of my sister nearly forty years after the event. With my assistance, he was subsequently released from prison because he had not committed this crime. A short while after he was released and thanked me publicly for my part in the verdict being quashed, he was arrested for causing the death of Nigel Ricketts by dangerous driving, failing to stop, failing to report an accident, and everything else that the Crown Prosecution Service could throw at him. This time, it was a crime that he most definitely did commit.

The reason that this all came to light as I have already indicated was that Steve Gregson had become my second husband. I was astonished when I came across his family's surname in the diary and passed it over for him to read to confirm what Gianna had written. When he read Gianna's diary, he remembered the incident very vividly—I suppose that isn't very surprising. He too was absolutely astonished to find his family name turn up in the diaries of my sister.

We went to the police, firstly in Venice where we live, and afterwards we flew to London with the diaries and all the details. We were assisted by Steve's friend at the Questura, Commendatore Franco Russo. I am always very wary of this particular gentleman, as is my daughter Maddalena, because we covered up information during the investigation of three murders in Venice, which we quite unwittingly became involved in. I am sure he still believes that we were economical with the truth (and he is right about that), but I hope that his obvious friendship with my husband allows him to forgive us. The press got hold of this story and had an absolute field day with it.

Steve's recollections and the diary record got the case reopened. I think the expression you use in English is "It's a small world," and in addition, perhaps, "Rough justice." Steve had been within a short distance from my sister all those years ago and fate decided that he should meet and marry me some forty years or so later. I showed him pictures of Gianna from about that time but he said that he couldn't honestly say that he remembered her. After all, she had been disguised, her hair would have been different, and her face partially covered. Miles Wilson, when confronted, admitted the crime and was sentenced to five years. As he was already in his late seventies, it seemed likely that he would only serve a fraction of that custodial sentence because he was not in very good health. Just so, he died in prison a few weeks later.

Steve's dark humour surfaced when he heard that Miles had died. "Shock from finally getting caught, I guess. Hope he didn't ask for his £2,000 back before he died!" I knew I could rely on him to say something like that.

The media interest in the story continued, and I received a very large offer from two Sunday newspapers in England and another in Italy that wanted to publish the diaries. The diaries were absolute dynamite, but there was no question of agreeing to that, whatever they offered, because I didn't want the private details of my family splashed all over the press. The newspapers also wanted to get the story from Steve's perspective. Again the bait was a large amount of money, but he resisted this on principle.

When I got to know him before we were married, he always expressed a deep contempt for the majority of journalists, particularly those who worked for the tabloids. The reason for this was that they had once run a story on his brother Christopher, who was a wealthy businessman. He said that the story was totally inaccurate and what they did not know, they made up. This resulted in a totally distorted picture and made his brother look terrible in the eyes of all who read it. It also upset his elderly mother, who was very distressed by the way her son was unfairly portrayed.

No wonder with this experience added to my reluctance, overall we came to the conclusion that we just wanted to be left in peace and the diaries were far too personal, not to mention too shocking, for the contents to be shared with anyone else. Steve was contacted by both of his brothers, who agreed likewise not to talk to the press. They were very pleased that the hit-and-run killer of their friend had at last been brought to justice. This was no consolation to the parents of Nigel Ricketts; both had passed on many years before, much to the chagrin of the hacks trying to chase down the story.

But this event and its long-term consequences was not all that happened in the fateful year of 1966. After the re-election of the Labour government, with a large working majority of over ninety seats, the country started to become gripped with a fever surrounding the football World Cup that was being held in England. It wasn't quite the same hysteria that you witness today; in those days there were only sixteen teams competing in the finals. Gianna clearly was not impressed because, as I have already indicated, she hated football. The principle reason for this was because of my father's slavish devotion to the game.

Carlo was interested as ever, as was his brother, Ronnie. His devotion to the game was an outlet for his hooliganism as a younger man, and it had landed him in trouble several times. Gianna couldn't stand him at any price. He worked for Carlo at the gallery, where he was employed as a caretaker and general handyman. He had served a prison sentence for manslaughter but was now, according to Carlo, a reformed character. An accident at birth had caused some brain damage when Ronnie was born. This tended to make him a bit of a social misfit. Carlo did as much as he could for his unfortunate brother and was repaid by his slavish devotion and loyalty. His manners and language were very coarse, but it was clear that he idolised Carlo and would do anything he asked of him.

One morning in the run-up to the opening of the tournament, Gianna called in at the gallery to see when Carlo wanted her to be in attendance because an exhibition and sale was soon to be held. Ronnie saw her, said good morning to her, and tried to further engage her in conversation.

"Your country's in it," he exclaimed loudly, "you know, Italy." He pronounced it "*It – a – lee.*"

Gianna was genuinely at a loss to understand what the hell it was he was going on about and, with a confused look on her face, replied, "I am sorry, I don't know what you mean, Ronnie."

"In the World Cup. You won't be able to see them, though—they're playing up north. It'll be on the telly though. You know something, the Italians might just win it." Gianna was not impressed and remained stoney-faced.

"Ronnie, I am not interested at all in football, in fact I hate it."

This threw Ronnie into confusion. To his way of thinking, this was a silly thing to say. How could anybody hate football? Women, he supposed, don't play football, and only a few, in his experience, ever went to watch it. Still, he persisted.

"Why do you hate it?"

"Ronnie, you wouldn't understand." Gianna had already had enough of this conversation, and it annoyed her still more when he later tried to tell her Italy's results after every game. He obviously had not gotten the message or was trying to make her interested. Italy performed poorly in the tournament, getting eliminated rather surprisingly by North Korea, who played against them in the group stages along with Chile and the Soviet Union. To the majority of Italians, the team were regarded as a national disgrace for the abject way that they played against the least fancied team in the whole tournament, but Gianna couldn't have cared less about it. Ronnie just couldn't leave it alone and persisted with his attempts at engaging his sister-in-law in conversation.

"Your team's in trouble when they get home," he gloated with a knowing tone in his voice. "I wouldn't like to be one of them!"

Gianna walked past him, totally ignoring him, and went into Carlo's office.

"Carlo, can you get your brother to shut up about this football World Cup? I am not interested in it. Apparently, Italy has lost a big game, but this is of no interest to me.

He keeps on going on about it—and most of the time, I don't understand anyway." She found that Carlo was in peacemaking mood.

"He's harmless, Gianna. He thinks you know about it because when he met your father at the wedding, it was the only thing that they had in common, not that they could understand a single word that was spoken. I spent a little time translating what they were saying. That is until I got fed up with it as well! Just smile at him and walk on."

Carlo was tolerant of his brother but Gianna found him tiresome and hated being in his company. She particularly resented it when he called around to the apartment in Mayfair at all hours. She didn't like him turning up without being invited, and it got to the stage that if she knew he was going to be there, then she would arrange to go out. Carlo mounted the usual defence of his brother when Gianna next complained about him.

"You are being harsh, Gianna. Ronnie means no harm. Sometimes he needs reassurance and pointing in the right direction."

"Well, I don't like the way he speaks, and perhaps you haven't noticed, he always has his hands in his pockets and is fiddling around with himself."

"Yes, I've told him not to do that but I'm afraid it's a habit. He has never had any contact with the opposite sex as far as I am aware but he thinks a lot about sex because he buys those awful magazines."

This brought back some unpleasant memories to Gianna but she wasn't prepared to listen to Carlo's excuses.

"Well, I'm not prepared to sit and watch him doing it. It is most off-putting."

Throughout the rest of July, the tournament was played, and much to the nation's delight, especially Ronnie, England won the World Cup. It was the reason for another party, and Gianna saw Miles for the first time since her mission over in West Dulwich following the hit-and-run fatality back in March some four months earlier. He had simply disappeared off abroad for a few months, combining work with a long vacation. He missed most of the summer season in London and must have felt he needed to be out of the way. He looked sheepish but summoned the courage to come over and speak to her.

"Did you, you know, get it delivered okay?" He asked this question nervously, already knowing the answer.

Gianna gazed back at him in disbelief at what she considered to be the stupidity of the question. "No, Miles, I spent the money on myself." He looked puzzled for a moment before it dawned on him that Gianna was having a wicked joke at his expense. "Yes, of course I did, didn't you see the headlines in the papers at the time about the mystery donor?"

"Yes, yes, of course. I have been away, you know, a bit out of touch. Good, good, honour satisfied, then?" He asked this as if he was trying to gain her approval as well as assuaging his own conscience.

"Well, not really. I played my part but it was you who killed the boy, not me." Miles, clearly agitated, glanced nervously around himself. "It's okay, Miles—no one can hear us."

He still wanted her attention.

"Look, Gianna, I want to talk to you about that and other things as well. Can we meet up again very soon? Here is not the place to have a discussion."

Gianna agreed, and they met two days later.

"I want you to divorce Charles and come and live with me," Miles said. "If you do, I promise that I will go to the police and confess to the manslaughter of that boy. There will be no need to say that you were in the car with me. I have a lawyer who will be able to get me a suspended sentence, I'm sure. It will all be sorted out. Then I want us to be married. I have the financial means to support you—whatever it takes. I have had bags of time to think about this while I have been away, and I have been through hell not having seen you."

The onslaught is over, thought Gianna. It sounded desperate and not a little embarrassing to be on the receiving end of this. She found it difficult to look him in the eye. "I cannot agree to what you are suggesting, Miles."

"Why not?"

"Firstly because I don't love you, and secondly I don't want to divorce Carlo. Thirdly, of course you can't hang a promise to do the right thing around whether I say yes or no to you. In any case, I don't think you are thinking straight. If you confess now it will open up the investigation again, and as an associate, I might be identified as the person who delivered the package. No—the time to admit to it was then, not now."

Miles looked downcast. "Okay, I accept what you are saying about that is right. But does it mean that you will never consider making your life with me?"

"Miles, I can't." Miles looked back at her glumly as she continued, "Look, why don't you hang on to what you have got? Let's face it, you have literally gotten away with murder; you'll have to live with the consequences, of course, but don't expect me to be dragged any further into your world of deception. We can see one another from time to time, but don't ask any more of me than that."

Miles felt well and truly put in his place but that is what he reluctantly settled for: a little piece of Gianna from time to time whenever he could get it.

Summer passed into autumn, and on the twenty-first of October, Gianna was at home when some dreadful news came on the radio that there had been a major incident in South Wales. Carlo had come home at lunch time from the gallery. It had been a quiet morning.

"Carlo, please listen to this." He listened attentively to the radio. A coal slagheap had slipped down the hill into the mining village of Aberfan, and the brunt of the landslide had been absorbed by the local primary school, which had been engulfed; there had been many fatalities. Carlo stayed and listened to the report as the news became clearer and shook his head in disbelief and disgust. "What would have caused that to happen?" Gianna asked, not fully taking in the detailed technicalities of the report.

"Well, as the reporter says, it was heavy rain on an unstable surface that caused the spoil from the pit to slide down the valley. Sounds like neglect to me by the

Coal Board people." He went on, "Typical of a bloody nationalised industry, if you ask me. I am afraid that life is full of this type of accident that people say will never happen, and we must learn lessons from it. What it really boils down to is, if people did their jobs properly in the first place, then these things would be much less likely to happen. I just hope someone is held to account." This was now turning into a full-scale rant. "I'd better get back to the gallery before I really lose my temper. I'll see you later." Carlo, genuinely troubled by what had happened that day, turned his gallery into a collection point for donations to the disaster appeal fund.

The following Friday, Gianna found herself in the gallery helping Carlo out prior to a new exhibition and showing Hayley Smith around, as it was likely that she would soon be coming to work in the gallery. Much to her discomfort, she was in the same room as Ronnie and an uncouth young man, not much older than herself, who looked like a weasel. His name was Brian Josephs, and he spoke with this unpleasant-sounding south London accent. He was short, wiry, but strong and had his dark hair greased back just like a pimp. After a while of being there, he broke wind very loudly and then twice more. On finishing his morning tea, he then burped loudly and then again. It was revolting but he obviously thought that it was clever to draw attention to himself in this way just by the way he spoke about it.

"Sorry, Ron, I'm fuckin' windy today, aren't I? Can't 'elp it, must 'ave been that Chinese meal I had last night after the beer. It was prawn something or other and some other bollocks. It tasted all right but now it's starting to come through. Won't stop gassing you out til I've 'ad a good shit."

He was helping Ronnie move heavy display items in and out of the gallery, and when he rested between shifting stuff, he took the opportunity to stare at Gianna and Hayley as they were working on some of the displays. Moments later, they overheard his conversation with Ronnie: "Cor, bloody hell, Ron—you seen that in there? Wouldn't mind getting up those two!"

Ronnie gestured with both hands for him to keep his voice down.

"Watch yourself, Brian—that's Charlie's missus and her mate. Anyhow, they're both too stuck up for someone like you, especially with all that farting you do, you dirty smelly bastard."

"Oops, sorry, Ronnie, didn't mean it. Still, I never seen such lovely tits in all my life as on the foreign one."

"Ssssh! Keep your voice down! That's Charlie's missus you're talkin' about."

"Your bruv is a lucky man. I'll 'ave the other one instead, she'll do. Anyway 'ave you 'eard the latest joke?" He was looking at one of the disaster appeal posters that had been put up in the gallery, and it was this that had triggered his memory.

"What's that then?"

"What's black and goes to school?" Brian waited a couple of seconds before supplying the punch line to the joke, which Ronnie had obviously not heard before. "A coal tip." Ronnie guffawed with laughter. "That's a wicked one, innit?" There were more jokes to follow on the same theme of the Aberfan disaster, and they were all in bad taste.

Gianna shuddered in disgust, as she had heard on the radio that morning the death toll in the disaster had risen to 144, with 116 of these being children. Hayley was likewise offended, and Gianna tried unsuccessfully to restrain her from walking down the room and remonstrating with him. Hayley confronted him with her nostrils twitching with disgust. She had walked into the foul smell of Josephs's almost continuous wind emissions. "We've had quite enough of that, thank you. We don't want to hear any more of your disgusting attempts at humour and revolting noises. You really are the limit."

"Oops, sorry, me lady." Josephs's response was in the accent of Parker, the character who was the chauffeur of posh Lady Penelope in the puppet-show "Thunderbirds." This disrespectful and feeble attempt at humour was not lost on Hayley, who realised that she was being sent up for having an upper class accent.

"Don't be so impertinent, you horrid little man."

Ronnie intervened in an agitated voice, worried by the fact that this incident might get back to Charlie. Brian had gone too far. "Sorry, miss. He means no harm; just gets carried away a bit."

Hayley turned away in disgust to rejoin Gianna further down the exhibition room. In the distance, she could hear Josephs breaking wind again and laughing. It was not possible to have any effect on a crude, ill-educated individual like Josephs, who still wasn't done yet with being as disgusting as he could be.

"'Ere Ron, think I've changed my mind about 'aving her, seein' as she don't appreciate my sense of humour. Can't please 'em all, can yer?"

As Ronnie feared, Gianna later recounted the incident to Carlo, making references to the coarse sexual comments made about them both, the impolite noises from both ends, the disgusting commentary on his bowel movements, and the awful jokes. Carlo shook his head as he listened to her outpouring of anger and said, "Oh, that is Brian Josephs—he does odd jobs for me now and then; take no notice of him, he's a moron. I should explain that when Ronnie spent time inside, Brian was very good to him. They were fellow inmates, so I hope that shows you what you're dealing with."

"Yes, well, your brother certainly seems to like him and also likes his jokes. He is very rude, and the jokes he told were terrible and disrespectful. Is that the so-called wonderful British sense of humour?"

"No, it isn't, Gianna. It's what we call sick humour, and it has become something of a cult thing in this country. People make jokes about things that are not funny, including people with disabilities. I agree with you; it's not very nice." As if to emphasise the point, he mentioned that the other day he overheard some nasty jokes being made about spastics, but Gianna was not being diverted from her issue.

"What if something really nasty happened to someone in his family?"

"Yes, I know."

"Can't you get rid of him?"

"Well, he is only a casual, and I only use him on jobs that require a bit of brute force. As you can imagine, I don't hire him for his brains, but I can't sack him just because he has a sick sense of humour. Also I have to think of Ronnie—he has very few friends."

"That's a pity. What about his disgusting manners?"

"Yes, I'm sorry. I'll have a word with both of them about that. Give my apologies to Hayley. It won't happen again. They need to show more decorum."

"I hope you don't use that word on *them*—they won't know the meaning of it!"

But a few days later, on the fourth of November, disaster struck, not the life of Brian Josephs, but the people of Venice. A combination of torrential rain and very strong winds stopped the morning tide from leaving the lagoon. When the afternoon tide came in, it caused the city to be flooded to a depth of over two metres above the normal water level—unprecedented in Venetian history. The tidal difference is usually less than half a metre because the city is protected by the outer islands in the lagoon, and Mediterranean tides are not great anyway. The city has always been subject to flooding but these were freak conditions. The water stayed for two days, and when it left, the city was a desolate place full of rubble, debris, and in places a thick black sludge from underground oil tanks that had simply burst. Dead pigeons floated on top of the disgusting water. The electricity went out, and for a while communications were very difficult. Fortunately, no one was killed in the floods but many lives and livelihoods were ruined.

The clean-up started immediately as the government and overseas charities came to the aid of the city. Carlo loved Venice and was devastated by the news, but his first concern was for Gianna's family. I think he was even more devastated by the news that came in from the city of Florence, which was likewise flooded, only worse. Parts of that city were a staggering seven metres under water, more than one hundred people lost their lives, and parts of the country's artistic heritage were lost forever. Gianna was only worried about me and would not have grieved if Papa had downed in the floods. Carlo, with his usual generosity, gave money to the disaster appeal fund and became actively involved in what was later to be known as the "Venice in Peril Fund." Posters of Venice under floodwaters replaced the appeal for aid at Aberfan.

He tried to persuade us to come to London for Christmas but Gianna was against this (without voicing her opposition too loudly). Back in Venice after the trauma, we didn't want to leave our home at all despite the fact that the city had been devastated. I was half persuaded but my father was very much against it. Funnily enough, it would have suited Gianna for just me to be there because she would have loved to show me around all the places she knew. But it was the way I felt, and by now I had sensed the change in her, the way she spoke and the decline in the number of letters I received. I was, at sixteen, not all that outgoing in personality and still quite shy when meeting new people. I thought I might struggle visiting London. So the answer to Carlo was politely but emphatically in the negative.

Carlo still wanted to do something to help and was very disappointed that we could not be persuaded. "It's a shame they won't come," he said. "I will wire some money to your father instead. At least that will cheer him up."

"That is not as good an idea as you think, Carlo."

"Why isn't it?"

"It will be spent on the three 'Ps': *prosecco, pornografia, e una prostituta*." Carlo did not need any translation and knew full well what she meant, but he had never really gotten to the bottom of Gianna's deep loathing of her father because she refused to tell him.

"You always think the worst of him. I know you don't want to tell me why but whilst I don't know the basis of the contempt you have for him, I have to speak as I find. I know he drinks a fair amount, but thinking about it so do I; you imply that he enjoys pornography; well, most men are guilty of looking at pictures like that from time to time; I admit to you also that as a young man, I used the services of a prostitute." He allowed this revelation to sink in before resuming.

"It was in Amsterdam and is one of the most shameful things I have ever done, and I really regret it. So perhaps I am not so very much different from him."

"You are simplifying it—you don't know him as I do. Send the money to Luisa instead—she has to put up with him at home and has inherited the work that I had to do for all those years. At least Mamma Isabella is not around anymore, so she does not have to deal with that."

"I'll send some to each of them." If Carlo had waited for her approval in the form of words, then he would have been there forever because he didn't receive it.

I remember receiving the money, and when in my delight I mentioned it to Papa, I also recall that he denied getting any, but that was more than likely because he didn't want anyone to know that his son-in-law was rich. He never told anyone that Carlo had funded the renovation of the property. This was because he liked to give the impression to his friends in the bar that he had this amazing job and earned a fortune. The gift sent would help to support that lie and the alter ego he tried so hard to promote and cultivate.

Back in England, before the year was out, there was a report on the news that a dangerous criminal had escaped from the remote Dartmoor prison in Devon on 12 December. He was Frank Mitchell, known as "the Mad Axeman." There was nothing so significant about this at the time, apart from the fact that the whisper was he had been sprung from prison by Ronnie and Reggie Kray. This was another piece of information Gianna had written in her diary (and no doubt stored away in her memory as well). She asked Carlo whether he believed that the Krays were really involved. It was New Year's Eve and they were getting ready to go out; Gianna noticed that Carlo was visibly troubled by the rumours and after not initially responding to her question, he volunteered a reply:

"You know, I am beginning to think that you are right about not going to the Krays' clubs any more. I think they are now completely out of control."

Their involvement in the Dartmoor story turned out to be true. Ronnie and Reggie also arranged for the Mad Axeman to be gotten rid of when he later became a bit of a nuisance, a murder that "Brown Bread" Fred Foreman later claimed to have carried out as a contract killing.

CHAPTER 11

Return Visits

Sooner or later, Gianna had to return to Venice, but it wasn't until well after the New Year. She was very reluctant to go, and only when Carlo said that they would be staying at the Gritti Palace did her resistance finally weaken and her spirits rise. Under no circumstances would she consider staying even for one night at the apartment in the company of Papa, and in fact she stated that if it was at all possible, she would not see him at all. Carlo was still puzzled by this continued hatred for her father and commented, "My goodness, Gianna, that is some loathing."

Gianna responded coolly, "He is some bastard." However, Gianna did end up seeing Papa and even managed to join in a few of the conversations that Carlo had with him (and me, of course). In the evening, Carlo went to all of his favourite restaurants and was also able to call upon a large number of friends and acquaintances. When he was entertaining or being entertained by people Gianna didn't like or found boring, she would go off on her own, and I know she spent quite a bit of time visiting old girlfriends like Alessandra and Carla.

"Why don't you bring your sister along, Gianna?" Carla asked with a glint in her eye. "My sister Anita really fancies her."

Gianna waved her hand dismissively. "She's wasting her time. Luisa is surrounded by boys most of the time and likes the attention she gets from them."

"Yes," mused Carla, "and I imagine she can afford to be very choosy indeed."

Alessandra wanted to move the conversation on. "Come on; tell us more about London and what you get up to."

It was over two years since Gianna had moved from Venice to London, and the stories of her new lifestyle left the two girls absolutely astonished. She let her small audience know that under no circumstances was she likely to return and live there permanently for at least another five years. "When you two finish University, you will have to come to London for a break, and I will show you around. We'll go to all the places you shouldn't go!"

The excited talk continued until they exhausted themselves. Eventually, the girls left her, and Gianna looked out of the window of the café where she was now seated alone in Campo San Bartolomeo on the San Marco side of the Rialto Bridge. It was one of those days in Venice when the mist rolled in off the lagoon, and although it was not raining yet, the city dripped with condensation from the cold. Already she was missing London and would be relieved to return there. Venice was still being cleared up and cleaned up after the great flood, and there was still a massive amount of work to be done. Would the city ever be rid of the background smell of decay?

Gianna was relieved to see that we, or should I say just I, seemed to be in no apparent danger from the disaster that had taken place. I sensed that she felt a bit guilty about not having seen me sooner. She called me up and insisted on taking me out shopping. We spent a lovely day out in Vicenza, which was a nice break away for me. We took an early morning train from Santa Lucia and talked all the way through the journey. When we got there, she bought me some fine new clothes, and we had a pleasant lunch together in the main Piazza dei Signori. When we got back home that evening, we went out to a restaurant, where she also insisted on paying.

For the next few days, this became the pattern. It was like she was trying to make up for all the lost time she should have had with me. One evening, I asked her and her friends to come around to the apartment because I wanted to make them dinner. I was determined to show how clever I was but still needed her assistance in the kitchen, otherwise I think I might have become overwhelmed by the occasion. Even though the main dish was only *risi e bisi,* it was a very successful evening, and the girls loved it. It occurred to me that I was the only one in the apartment out of six that night who was not bisexual or a lesbian. I was also aware of the fact that amongst them, I now had a number of admirers, but none of them made any advances on me that evening.

Following that evening, it was soon evident that Gianna was getting bored with being back at home in Venice, and I sensed that she was very glad to be going back to London soon. I had seen Carlo three times during this visit, and as always, he paid me an enormous amount of attention. Before he went back, he gave me a large sum of money in lire and insisted that I buy something really nice for myself. I tried not to accept it but he would not allow me to return it to him, and in addition, he made me promise to come to him if ever I was in trouble and needed help.

The next time Carlo went to Venice, in the early spring, he could not persuade Gianna to go with him. He was very disappointed but she still remembered the smell of the city from the last visit and could not be tempted. Instead, he took Hayley, who had now replaced Gianna at the London Gallery as the main administrator and public relations person, although Gianna still went in one day per week, which was Hayley's day off. As you are aware, Gianna actually recommended her for the job (an action that she sometimes regretted). It coincided with Gianna deciding not to see her anymore, and Hayley was absolutely devastated by the ending of their affair. Gianna found Hayley overpowering, always trying to make her do things she didn't want to and generally trying to control her life.

Being in her company also meant that at times she would have the unpleasant experience of seeing Cecil Smith. He would act as if she wasn't in the room, and when he thought she was out of earshot, he rudely referred to Gianna as "the spaghetti eater." Hayley had become obsessive and possessive in the same way as Miles, and Gianna, the embodiment of the free spirit, just couldn't take it any more.

The work that Carlo was doing now involved more frequent trips to Italy, not just Venice but also Florence, which was a city very close to his heart. He always visited us just the same, but now it was Hayley who accompanied him. She could not at first speak Italian, other than the odd word or two. This did not matter to Papa, with whom she got along very well. Gianna warned me that Hayley was coming, and when I asked her what she was like, she would not say and told me to decide for myself. I knew my sister well enough to deduce from this that she didn't like her for some reason.

My first impression was coloured by the fact that her fine legs were shown off by skirts that were very short and her fine breasts were displayed in tops that allowed everyone to see what was there. When I was close to her, I quite often noticed that her breath didn't smell very nice, as if she was having stomach trouble of some kind. She was a fussy eater and did not appear to like pasta very much, which is a big problem if you visit homes and restaurants in Italy. I found her very insincere, and I imagined she was one of these women who would use her sexuality as much as she could to gain attention and ultimately get her own way. Even though at that stage, I could not understand much English at all, she would use a babyish voice and flash her eyes at Carlo and Papa, who of course loved it. I had never witnessed antics like this before.

When I described her to my husband Steve, he said he knew the type of person I was describing, as he had worked with that kind before more than once. According to him, a woman like this will work her way into men's affections by playing on the fact that she is "only a woman" and doesn't know very much in this man's world that we are living in. It is submissive behaviour but masks the fact that there is a really lot of scheming going on. Steve calls them "fluffy bunnies," and when he did an impersonation of one, it reminded me so much of what Hayley was like when I first met her that it was uncanny. He went on to explain this:

"I used to share an office with a woman like that in the days when I was a college lecturer. Her name was Diana, and although she was a nice enough woman and very attractive, when she turned this behaviour on, it made you want to go and throw up. The other women despised her partly because she was better looking than all of them but mainly because they could see what her game was, which was to gain favour with her bosses or senior colleagues—anyone who had the power to advance her career. She never dressed like Hayley but she was a nervous type, always worrying about something, and strange to mention this, when you got close to her she also had bad breath—perhaps to do with nerves, anxiety, and such like. Funnily enough, it was also rumoured that she put it about a bit, but I was never too sure about that."

"I am sorry, Steve," I said (I was lost, not for the first time, by his use of language), "I don't understand this saying 'put it about a bit.'"

"It usually means having sex with a number of men."

"I see. Including you, I expect." I enjoyed teasing him like this.

Now he felt it necessary to cover his tracks.

"No, like I say, I don't think she did because she was married herself, already on husband number two, as it happened. Anyway, I was already married and resisted the temptation to get involved, even though she did once suggest it in a roundabout sort of way." He stopped for a moment to reflect on the past and then quickly added, "Besides which, Samantha would have killed me if she found out that I had gotten involved with another woman."

I knew and remembered Sam very fondly and was sure that this was true. I looked at him, and he could see that I was smiling at him, but he didn't understand that he had amused me. "What's the matter?" he asked.

"Nothing. Go on, I'm listening to your story."

"Anyway, as I was saying, initially I helped her quite a lot with her work because I was what they called a course team manager and she was a part of my team of lecturers. She played up to me for a while, and I suppose it was quite good for my ego to be flattered in this way. But I noticed she would drop people who were no longer useful to her. She would also tell tales on other members of staff, pointing out their weaknesses and deficiencies, which wasn't a very nice thing to do in an environment that required teamwork. I got fed up with her because I found that her work with the students was not up to standard. Her classes would finish too early, and students were making a lot of negative comments about her. You have to be careful not to go too much by what students say at times but when the good ones start making complaints, then it is time to do something.

She got very defensive about this when she got pulled up, and at the end of the academic year, I reviewed the stuff she was doing. I took her off the more important subjects when I came to the conclusion she couldn't teach them properly. She didn't like this, and it got worse for her when I only gave her stuff to teach that was not easy to mess up. Eventually, she became a marginal figure on my team, and I stopped having much to do with her after a couple of quite severe disagreements. Most of the students ended up hating her as well. So she had to go and play the 'fluffy bunny' elsewhere in the College, which of course she did."

I was now in no doubt what being a "fluffy bunny" meant, and I hope that you also get the picture—these were just the same characteristics of Hayley Smith, and during the course of the year that followed, I got used to her visiting the apartment, but I didn't look forward to her being there. For Papa, read the opposite of the feelings I am expressing. He loved it when she was there and would play up to her, especially when her Italian language skills improved and she could join in on the conversational banter.

Hayley thought it would be a good idea to try and make Gianna jealous. She would telephone her at home. "I am going away with Charles again to the Galleria in Venice," she said provocatively. "They are getting quite used to me turning up, and last time one of the new officials, who doesn't know you, thought I was his wife. Perhaps I should say that I am."

In a disinterested voice, Gianna replied, "Yes, perhaps you should. Is that the only reason you phoned me? It makes no difference to me, Hayley, what you do anymore." She replaced the receiver before Hayley could say anything in reply.

But Hayley was to have the last word. When she came back from the latest trip, she telephoned my sister. "Gianna, I am just phoning you to let you know that I have finally given up on you. Also I am sorry to say that your husband is a perfect gentleman. Not once has he made a pass at me or said anything remotely inappropriate, but I'll tell you something—it was great fun having sex with your father, as pleasurable as it used to be with you, only slightly different."

Gianna could just imagine her gloating face as she said it, but her only response was to replace the telephone receiver and try and block out what she had just heard. That would be typical of her father, who would use her like he used other women, only this time he didn't have to pay for what he was getting.

Hayley was no longer part of her social circle, and she had recently taken up with another girlfriend from the group. Her full name was Joanna Jessica Price-Ward, which led to her being called J-J or Jo-Jo, which she preferred. At one party, which was not attended by Carlo, who was away, Jo-Jo invited Gianna to stay overnight. Gianna pointed out that Jo-Jo's husband Rick was around and perhaps it wasn't such a good idea. Jo-Jo replied by saying that it didn't matter because he thought Gianna was absolutely gorgeous. She added flippantly, "He won't mind as long as he gets to watch."

Gianna said she wasn't sure about that but needn't have worried because, as it turned out, Rick got so drunk he fell asleep on the sofa before the two of them disappeared up to the bedroom. He was still fast asleep when Gianna disappeared out of the door the next morning. According to Jo-Jo, he was furious that he had missed the action.

Gianna's other married friend was Susan Templeman. Gianna liked her enormously and was quite disappointed to find out that she was straight, but she accepted it without making a nuisance of herself. Susan's problem was that she had affairs with other men, mainly because Harry, her husband, was disinterested in sex and not very interested in anything other than making money on the stock market. He was twenty years older than Susan and firmly belonged in that generation that seemed to be rooted totally in the period of the Second World War, when he was a member of the ground crew for the RAF. It was still present in the old-fashioned language he used, almost as if he was still there fighting it. Carlo used to make fun of him and call him "Green Light and Bandits at Four O'clock." Harry Templeman was a bore but one of the very few who could tolerate Cecil Smith, who was also a crashing bore, and now that he was out of the circle, he had no one to talk to on social occasions. He had absolutely no idea that his wife was carrying on affairs.

Susan used the same escort agency as Andrea Hannington. One day, Gianna let her know that she was having trouble with Miles Wilson, and Susan suggested that she should use the same agency to date young men. If Miles, who Susan couldn't stand at any price, continued to stalk her, then he would see Gianna out with younger men and perhaps lose interest.

"Gianna, darling, the agency seems to come up with some absolutely gorgeous young men. I think they must have to pass some kind of screen test. Judging by the ones I've been out with, they must measure them for size down there in the tool box department before they take them on."

Gianna was amused by this description and started to use the agency. Not all the encounters ended up in a sexual relationship, as it was completely up to the client. She took to one of the younger men, named Gerry Stevens, who likewise became interested in her. He would escort her out quite often, and from that an affair started, and they soon started seeing one another without going through the agency. This was against the rules, of course, but Gianna never played by anyone's rules but her own unless it suited her purposes.

One evening, she was out with him having a drink in the Cockney Pride theme pub in Piccadilly, which was a brash modern invention that very soon went out of fashion. The idea was to try and create the atmosphere of the past, but any degree of authenticity was spoilt by the inclusion of brightly flashing gaming machines. She felt it was unlikely that anyone from her circle would go there but she noticed Miles in the shadows, up to his old tricks. So, well done, Susan; this gave her the chance that she was waiting for. She sat down in one of the alcoves and could see Miles out of the corner of her eye. He had his evening newspaper again, his standard prop, it seemed, for stalking her. Knowing that she was in his line of sight, she leaned over and, much to the surprise (and no doubt delight) of Gerry, gave him a very long French kiss, with her tongue exploring his mouth. When she had finished, it was quite difficult for her to keep a straight face because Gerry looked absolutely stunned.

"That was for being so nice to me. I hope you have some johnnies with you tonight." Gianna said this quite loudly, and a very pleased-looking Gerry, slightly embarrassed, patted his pocket in confirmation.

"Keep the volume down a bit, Gianna, I think some people might have heard that," he said with a smile.

She reached across, looking deeply into his eyes, and held both of his hands; she said to him quietly, "Gerry, there is a man over in the corner just out of sight from you who is stalking me, and I want him to see that I am no longer interested in him. I used to go out with him on a regular basis; now lean over and kiss me again. I want it to look like we are very much in love."

Once again, this was no problem for Gerry. A couple of minutes later, Gianna could see the back of Miles retreating out of the pub door. "It's okay now, he has given up and gone." She was having fun and it showed. "I hope you didn't mind doing that in such a public way."

"Glad to be of service, madam," Gerry said, joining in with the spirit of the occasion. Gianna enjoyed going out with young Gerry because he never made serious demands of her. He had only just turned twenty and had a girlfriend of his own, and he said she would go mad if she knew that he was seeing another girl.

"What is she like?"

"Well, she's very nice—we've been going out for about six months. It's nothing too serious—well, not as far as I am concerned, and put it this way, I don't think it will last forever. I have to say she is not really in your league."

"How old is she?"

"She's eighteen." *That was one year older than Luisa*, Gianna noted mentally. She had a feeling that Luisa would like Gerry.

"Bring her to the gallery if you like; I'd like to meet her. Remember, I am only there on Fridays. Now take me back home please."

"Don't you want to go on somewhere else, Gianna? It's still very early."

When they got back home to the apartment, she thanked him for playing his part so well in the pub and led him into the bedroom, where she showed her appreciation. Afterwards, he remarked that he could never remember a time when he had to do so little to gain so much pleasure.

"*Prego*," Gianna replied in her native tongue, and she put on her dressing-gown.

"I've heard you say that before. What does it mean again?"

"In English, it means don't mention it."

A couple of weeks later, Gerry turned up at the gallery. "Hello, Gianna, this is Gill. I thought we'd drop in. Gill's not long finished her 'A' levels, and I thought as we were up in town, it would be nice to drop in."

"*Buongiorno, Signorina Gill, come stai*? What are you studying?"

"Languages, but not Italian I'm afraid; French and German. I hope to read them at University." Gianna then started to speak to her in German, and they chatted away, which left Gerry floundering because his knowledge of the language was only rudimentary. Gianna explained that she could have gone to University but chose to go to work instead. Gill then said that Gerry could have gone to University also but there was family pressure for him to start earning a living, so he didn't go. She felt that it was a mistake not to go if you were good enough and were given the chance.

"Yes, but sometimes other things take over. I must say your German is very good, Gill."

"Thank you, I was lucky enough to go on an exchange for two summers running, in Hannover and then in Munich—it made a huge difference to me."

"That's fantastic—I bet you noticed the difference in dialect between those two places."

"Yes, at first I hardly understood a word when I went to southern Germany."

"German was always my second language at school; then I went to language school, and at home I would speak in German to my sister, who was also very good at it. We did it to annoy my father as well." They both laughed and now reverted to English, having sensed Gerry's discomfort at being left out.

"Gerry's not all that interested in art and knows nothing about it, so goodness knows what he finds to talk to you about."

"That's not entirely true," Gerry said. "I know what I like." He sensed that he was not convincing them and backed down. "Well, I suppose it is; it's the free coffee I like."

Gerry wandered off to look at some of the exhibits, and when he was out of earshot, Gill resumed her conversation with Gianna. Her facial expression changed.

"It's you he comes to see, isn't it? You're beautiful. He has told me about you, and I can tell that he is a bit infatuated with you."

"I've not noticed that. If that is the case, he is wasting his time. I'm married but I expect he has told you that; let me tell you a little secret." She leant over and whispered in her ear, "You are in more danger from me than he is."

Oh my God, Gill thought, *a lesbian*. It was not that she hadn't encountered lesbians before; there had been a few at school, but none of them had been attractive like this girl. In fact, to quote Gerry, they were all the dodgy girls who looked as if they had fallen out of the ugly tree.

"You mean you go with girls? But you are married." This was said with a tone of disbelief, but she had felt a mild frisson of excitement, and her cheeks flushed.

"Yes, so your boyfriend is doubly safe with me, but *you* can come and see me anytime."

Gill coloured up again and went off to find Gerry, and Gianna could only imagine the conversation that was now going on; she smiled inwardly. They left the gallery some twenty minutes later, and Gianna noticed Gill pick up a publicity leaflet, which contained contact telephone numbers. *I bet she phones me,* thought Gianna.

Gerry's next meeting with Gianna was quite interesting; she asked, "What did your pretty little girlfriend say about me?"

"She said that you were a lesbian."

"And what did you say to that?"

"I said it was legal."

Gianna laughed. "Anything else, or is that it?"

"She said that it was just as well for me that you are one because you are way out of my league, and I would be wasting my time."

"But that is what you said about her!"

"Touché."

The following week, Gianna got a call whilst she was at the gallery. It was from Gill, and they arranged to meet up. Apparently, she was curious to know what it was like to go with a girl, and it was from Gianna that she found out. It was an experience she appeared to enjoy. She said that she had found sex with Gerry painful because he was so big, and because of this, she was put off by the prospect of long-term relationships with boys.

Gianna remembered that Gerry was quite large. "It is something that in time you get used to. You must learn to relax, take your time, and tell him what you like and don't like."

The irony of this meeting was that she begged Gianna not to tell Gerry about them sleeping together. If it were possible, Gill would have stayed all weekend but Gianna had to send her home with a promise they would soon meet again. Then she teased her by saying she would tell Gerry if she didn't come back and see her again.

The next time Carlo said he was going to Venice, Gianna said, "This time I will come with you, because I want to see my sister. Don't take that assistant of yours because she will get in the way."

Carlo was taken by the surprise of her announcement and the vehement tone, and although he already knew the answer to the question, he still asked, "You mean Hayley, the person you recommended to me?"

"Yes, that's right."

"You don't want her cramping your style, is that it?" She could tell that Carlo was teasing her. "She always speaks very highly of you. Did you know that? At one time, you were pretty much inseparable; what went wrong?"

"She is not all she seems to be."

"A favourite saying of yours, I have come to notice. Well, we can all be guilty of that from time to time." This was said in a very even tone, and Carlo then reinforced what he was saying by staring Gianna directly in the eye.

"I think we should all make sure that our own houses are in order."

Gianna remained cool, and her face betrayed nothing, but inside she wondered how much he knew about the other life she had been leading.

"Yes, you are right," she said finally, and in an attempt to deflect the underlying criticism that she sensed was present in his remark, she added, "and let's begin by spending more time together. I go out on my own too much; I know this, but there again, you are away much of the time and this means I can get bored."

"There's always work at the gallery."

"You would condemn me to working with your brother and the likes of Brian Josephs, such charming men. Then there is Hayley, whose company I can't stand. Thank you."

"Well, you could always find a job. You have your languages—a tremendous asset to any number of firms, as it has been to me up to now." Carlo was trying to sound encouraging but wasn't getting through to her.

"I don't want to spend all my time translating boring documents or acting as an interpreter, Carlo. For a while, your gallery events were good fun but your world is not my world."

"Well, what do you want, Gianna—to be a fashion model or such like?"

"Now you are making jokes and ridiculing me. I want the life you promised me when I left Venice."

"You mean *la dolce vita*. I think you already have that. I don't want to argue with you, but I must remind you that I still have to work. Perhaps I ought to set you up in business, doing something to keep you occupied.

I think your problem now is that you have no focus and you are not using your brain. I want you to have a good think about this and then tell me what you would like to do, and then I will see what can be done." Gianna remained silent. "But in the meantime, I think you should come back home to Venice and stay as long as you like. Come with me to the Galleria and see some of your old colleagues—they always ask after you. I think you need to get back into the world of art, even though you say it isn't your scene any more—you were very good at it, once upon a time."

"Perhaps," Gianna replied without very much conviction, because she had very different reasons for wanting to return to Venice. "But still, no Hayley please."

"As you wish."

There was a look of surprise on Papa's face when he opened the door to his elder daughter. Gianna had chosen a time when she knew that I would not be there. Papa did not really know what to say and sat down in his armchair, removing the cushion and throwing it on to the floor. "This is a rare visit. What is it you want?"

"I made a promise to myself that I would never be in the same room as you without at least one other person present, but your behaviour has made this visit necessary." Gianna looked around the room and noticed it was very neat and tidy. That would be the hand of her sister. "I see that Luisa keeps this place looking very nice."

He answered cautiously, still waiting to hear the real reason for her presence here. "Yes, your sister is a good girl.

There is no need for you to check up on me; what do you mean by my behaviour?"

"Yes, there is a need. You have resisted the urge to touch her so far." It was a statement of fact, not a question.

Papa became agitated, shifting in his chair. "What happened all those years ago was wrong, and I bitterly regret it."

"Yes, it showed you up for the pervert that you are, and let me remind you, it was only four years ago. To me, it seems like yesterday."

"Look, I can't change what happened, and I am ashamed of what I did. What more can I say?"

"Well, I suppose you could say that you were sorry for ruining my life, or perhaps even 'thank you' for not going to the police. You would have just finished your prison sentence by now if I had reported you." He remained silent. "Actually, I am here on another, not unrelated matter. I understand that you have turned your attention toward another girl who is young enough to be your daughter." He opened his mouth to speak but she continued before he could get the words out. "That is your business, and I don't really care. She told me because she wanted to make me jealous. You see, *we* had a relationship, which I finished. What I don't want her to know is what you did to me, because it will get back to Carlo and, in the end, to Luisa. I promise you that if I find out you have talked about this, I will ensure that it is the last thing you will do—the same as I threatened to do if I ever find you have touched Luisa."

"It is clear enough, but you must tell me, what are you going to do? Get a gun and shoot me or will it be a knife whilst I am asleep? Do I need to take out protection?"

148

Gianna knew she was being mocked and decided to scare him out of his wits. "Whilst I have been living in London, I have been introduced to many people. I get to meet all types in West End nightclubs when I am out with Carlo and his friends. Some of them come from the East End of London. This is a very rough part of London, with some very rough people. On the surface, they can appear to be quite charming, if a little coarse, but underneath they are not very nice at all. They can be as vicious and nasty as the *Mafioso*. Like them, they do anything illegal for money." She hoped this was sinking in, but wanted to make sure. She was referring to gangland killers like the Kray brothers. "You won't know your killers when they come." Papa's joking arrogance disappeared as he turned white and felt a cold shudder overtake his body. She got up to leave. "Enjoy your nights of passion with Hayley when you see her, Papa. I can tell you that lots of other men and women do; mind you don't catch something because she is not very fussy who she goes with—you, of course, being the best example that I can think of."

Papa was now angry. "Get out! I never want to see you again!"

"Don't worry, you won't. Just remember to keep your hands to yourself when you are anywhere near Luisa."

She picked up a cushion that was on the floor and threw at him. It missed him, and she walked quickly out of the apartment, closing the door firmly behind her. After this confrontation, Gianna felt much better about herself. She had not spoken like that to her father since her departure from Venice. That same day, she intercepted me as I was returning from school. I heard this voice calling to me in German: "*Can you pass me that bottle of olive oil please, Fraulein?"* It was one of the phrases from when we used to practice our language skills together, and straight away I knew who it was. I ran toward her and jumped all over her, nearly knocking her over. For a few minutes, there was an excited babble of conversation, during which Gianna persuaded me to come out with her after I had dropped my stuff off at home.

"Have you seen Papa?"

"Yes, I paid him a courtesy visit just now, but I won't do so again for a while. He and I don't get on, as you well know, but these days, let's just say we agree to disagree. It's best that we don't see each other." I nodded as she continued, "I will never forget his treatment of Mamma. What's he like to live with these days?"

"Well, as usual he is rarely home. This is okay because when he is around, he is untidy and doesn't know where anything is. It's 'Luisa, where's this? Luisa, where's that?' He is infuriating. He thinks I am bossy I'm sure, but as I look after the home, he has learned to do as he is told! I don't find him as bad as he used to be, but he still goes out and gets drunk and tries to act the big man that he would surely like to be. As long as he gives me the money for the household bills, then I can't really complain."

"He never bothers you in the way I warned you about?"

"No, I would tell you if anything like that happened. Also, I have never found any more of those horrible pictures."

"Good. Does he bring anybody home?"

"No, I won't allow it."

At this point, Gianna fell about, laughing. "Good for you, Luisa! I just love that! Wait until I tell Carlo!"

When I saw Papa following this conversation with Gianna, he was remarkably subdued for reasons that are now plain for me to see. I told him that I was going out with Gianna and that he would have to get his own dinner. I reminded him to clear up after he finished as I left to go out. I had a great night out with my sister, and we met up with some of her usual friends. Gianna walked me back until we were in sight of my front door, but when I got inside, the apartment was eerily quiet. I called out to see if Papa was in. Perhaps he had gone out to the bar. There was no smell of cooking, and everywhere was as neat and tidy as when I had left earlier in the evening, apart from the armchair where he had been sitting, which was untidy as usual. There was a note on the kitchen table in his usual scrawl. He had decided to leave early for a trade fair in Verona and would be away for a week. I thought that he was put out because I went out instead of attending to him. Good, it meant that Gianna could come and see me without having to be in his company at all.

Gianna stayed longer this time, and I really felt myself connecting with her again. It was like old times. Papa called to say he would be away for an extra week. I think he was telephoning from the house of this other woman he kept, who lived in Vicenza. I could hear another voice in the background whilst we were talking. The only problem for me was that when Gianna left for London, it was very hard saying good-bye. Although we spoke many times after her departure by telephone, it was the last time I was to see her alive. I still remember her lovely, smiling face as she waved to me as I stood on the quayside at San Zaccaria, as the boat took off on its journey across the lagoon to the airport. I still can't go by that spot without the tears welling up in my eyes, even to this day.

Carlo's other visits that year were always in the company of Hayley. Much as I tried, I found it very difficult to like her. It was about this time I first started to see my future first husband Dario Ongaro. He became a regular visitor, travelling from Treviso to spend time with me. I introduced him to Carlo and Hayley and was pleased to get out of the apartment with him so I didn't have to put up with Hayley's simpering and mothering behaviour. Dario was at first very shy and could not cope with my family situation very well. Carlo warned me about bossing him around too much, but I had gotten used to being like this because of the general uselessness of Papa in the domestic set-up.

In the meantime, Gianna was back in London, pursuing her hedonistic lifestyle. A few years before, in 1960, Federico Fellini's film *La Dolce Vita* had stunned and outraged the more conservative establishment in Italy. When I watched it again recently, it seemed quite tame by today's standards but it is not difficult to see how it might have offended people. Carlo made frequent reference to the fact that what my sister wanted was *la dolce vita*. He would say this in a joking manner. It is quite clear that in London, she associated with many of the types of people that were depicted in that film and became very decadent in their company as a result.

It is interesting in recent times to read many social commentators in Britain say 1960 marked the year that Queen Victoria finally died. I have already made reference to these changes, the most significant of which was the new era of sexual permissiveness, fuelled by the widespread availability of the contraceptive pill. Steve looks back on this time with some amusement, not to mention enjoyment. He insists that he was a late-sixties man and was not in on the change from the start but had, nonetheless, been dragged along by events. He lamely defends his stance by saying, "I was corrupted by other people. I tried hard to lead a blameless life but got carried away. It wasn't my fault."

I have come to appreciate the richness of the English language since I have known him, and Steve commented that Gianna was the kind of girl who used to "let it all hang out," a phrase coined in those times and still used quite frequently today. In Italy, this sexual revolution took a little longer to arrive. In Rome and in the north of Italy, it caught on much quicker than in the south.

Gianna continued to be pursued by the young, the not-so-young, the straight, and the gay. She also liked to generate the excitement. One evening, she invited both Gerry and Gill over to the apartment. Neither one knew that the other had been invited, because she asked them not to say anything. This was a wickedly playful thing to do, and it brought the three of them together with the inevitable result. It was a form of sexual experimentation that she had never tried before, and in my view it was ploughing the depths. But she didn't seem to care about this at all. It was reading this in her diary that made me come to the conclusion that she was totally out of control. The description of what went on was graphic, and I will not say any more, other than it involved three in a bed. I wonder what the experience did for the two younger people involved. She seemed able to detach herself and made it a rule never to become emotionally attached.

Most of the things she did were strictly on a business basis and carried out with the utmost discretion. The only people who had real problems in accepting this were Miles and Hayley (and ultimately, of course, Carlo). Gianna's problem was that she didn't know that Carlo had found out about her secret life, or at least some elements of it. It should come as no surprise to you that the person I suspect blowing the whistle on her activities was the scorned and vengeful Hayley. Gianna was always worried that this might happen and felt she lost control of the situation when Hayley revealed that she had started an affair with my father. It is possible that Carlo found out by other means, but I shall never really know for sure.

In the meantime, Venice started to go through a boom. Fears that the city might soon sink beneath the waves encouraged visitors from all over the world to come and take a look at it before it did. I was by now studying at University and having the time of my life. Dario was often very jealous of what went on, and at one point I thought he might break off our relationship. I refused to modify any of my social arrangements to accommodate his visits, which were difficult for him to arrange because he was undergoing training in the catering industry, which in Italy requires an extensive course of study.

The tourist office began recruiting linguists, and as I was now studying German, as well as Italian literature, and could speak the language quite fluently, I was sufficiently brave enough to apply for work as a guide. I passed the language test quite easily, but the bureaucratic formalities were more difficult than I expected because it involved becoming officially registered. Once this had been settled, they were very keen for me to take groups of Germans and

Austrians around the city. The route and script I worked to did not vary much, and as a native Venetian, knowing where everything was located, I found it quite easy. After a short time, I could do it without any kind of notes. I found the visitors very generous, and I made more from tips than the fees paid for guiding. I took Italian groups as well, but the Germans were more forthcoming with tips. You got the odd tourist who wanted to meet up with you afterwards but we were told that if we received unwanted attention, we had to say that it was against the rules and could lose our jobs. This explanation worked in 99 percent of cases.

The hotels, bars, and cafes all cashed in on this boom, and prices in the high season soared, making Venice one of the most expensive places to visit if you did not know your way around and past the tourist traps. At times, the Piazza San Marco was so heavily congested with tourists that it seemed that it might sink under their weight. So in both respects, nothing has changed much in the last four decades—Venice still gets overcrowded, and it is still very expensive for the visitor. My life was very busy, and I therefore did not resent it that Gianna now seemed reluctant to visit any more. We spoke quite regularly by telephone, and she was delighted when she learned that I had become a city guide.

Back in London, she had been taking driving lessons, and upon passing her test, Carlo bought her a brand new 1967 Mini Cooper S Mark II. It was blue with a white roof, and as it was her pride and joy, she wouldn't let anyone else drive it. I still have pictures of her posing beside it, wearing her sunglasses. There she was—Gianna Ambrosio-Court, an icon of the swinging sixties in

London. She had fog lamps fitted to the front grill of the Mini, and it was almost as if she liked to give the impression that she was going to enter the Monte Carlo Rally. Carlo joked that he didn't mind the expense just so long as she didn't think of graduating to something more expensive, like a Jaguar E Type.

In the meantime, her diaries continued to make references to the Kray brothers, and she now took to socializing with them without being in the company of Carlo. Carlo didn't like it that she sought their company and said so, but it made no difference. What he didn't know was that Ronnie was paying her money to bring in friends and friends of friends to gamble on his tables. These criminal activities continued, hidden behind their celebrity status and so-called legitimate businesses. In October 1967, four months after the suicide of his wife Frances, Reggie Kray was encouraged by his brother Ronnie to kill Jack (the Hat) McVitie, a minor member of the Kray gang who had failed to carry out a £1,500 contract paid to him in advance to kill a man named Leslie Payne. Payne had been the financial brain behind the Krays' business since the early 1960s, but it now looked as though he was going to do a deal with the police that involved shopping the Krays in return for immunity from prosecution. McVitie had not broken the contract but didn't want to be rushed in any way, preferring to do things in his own time. This drove Ronnie into a fit of temper.

Gianna described McVitie, whom she had the misfortune to meet, as an absolutely vile man and mentioned to Ronnie that his presence at the club was putting some of her friends off from coming. Ronnie said,

"Don't worry, Gianna, and just tell your nice friends that my associate Jack the Hat won't be around for very much longer."

McVitie, who had already been paid the contract money and gave no explanation for not carrying out the job, was lured to a basement flat in Evering Road, Hackney, on the pretence of a party. As he entered, Reggie Kray pointed a handgun at his head and pulled the trigger twice, but the gun failed to go off. Ronnie then held McVitie in a bear hug, and Reggie was handed a kitchen knife. He stabbed McVitie in the face and stomach, driving it deep into his neck, twisting the blade, continuing as McVitie lay on the floor dying. Several other members of the Kray gang, known as "The Firm," including the Lambrianou brothers (who initially made a mess of getting rid of the body), were convicted of this killing. McVitie's body has never been found to this day, and it was said that it ended up in one of the concrete pillars that support the motorway interchange at Spaghetti Junction near Birmingham. This is probably just an urban myth but the sort of story that the brothers liked to propagate.

Gianna had no doubt that Ronnie had ordered the killing. One day, he mentioned to her that McVitie had been killed in an accident so he wouldn't be troubling her nice friends any more.

CHAPTER 12

Downhill to Disaster

Some time in early 1968 is when I think that Carlo must have found out about the double life Gianna was leading (or more likely, had his earlier suspicions confirmed). I would not be surprised if it was Hayley who tipped him off in a roundabout sort of way, but again I can't be sure of that. It was certainly a fear that Gianna experienced, as it kept on appearing in the pages of the diary.

I would speculate that Carlo, once his suspicions were aroused, had her followed or stalked her himself. I have not discounted the possibility that Carlo discovered her diaries and gained a sense for himself what was going on, even though he didn't speak German at all well. They are highly explicit, and I admit that some of the entries made me cringe. I had been reading them on and off for a few days when I asked Steve to cast his eye over a few of the early pages that I had already browsed to see what his reaction was.

"My German isn't as good as yours," he pointed out, "so I might have to ask you the odd word or two." As it happened, his German is better than he gives himself credit for, and he only had to ask me twice about the grammatical sense and syntax of the text. He gave the diary back after about twenty minutes of study without saying anything at all to me. He has this habit of raising his eyebrows and then gently shrugging his shoulders in order to indicate his thoughts, especially when he doesn't want to say anything, but this time I wanted him to say something and pressed him.

"Well, what do you think? I mean on the basis of what you have just read."

He stopped and thought for a moment before replying.

"One of my favourite novelists about thirty-odd years ago was Len Deighton. He was absolutely brilliant and used to write these really good spy stories. The writing of the books overlapped with Ian Fleming's James Bond, only they were in my view better with far more believable stories. Anyway, the main character in one of his early books, *Funeral in Berlin*, came out with this kind of homespun philosophy about two types of woman you should never go out with. I may have this in the wrong order, but one is a woman who insists on telling you the truth, and the other is one who keeps a diary."

He paused for a moment to see if this was sinking in. It was starting to register—although I am getting better, I still find the nuances of the English language difficult at times.

"You mean if Carlo really did find the diary, then it would be very incriminating? Luckily he didn't speak German to a level that would make understanding easy."

"Thank goodness for that, because it would be very incriminating if he did speak German to any level. No listen, what Len Deighton was really saying in his book is that it can be very awkward and unpleasant for a man, or a woman for that matter, who is reminded of his or her failings either verbally or in written form. So don't go out with that sort of person!"

"That could mean that you end up with no one, surely." However, I could see what he was getting at, and this was before I reached the section when she started having an affair with Miles Wilson, so what Steve was saying at that stage was something of an understatement.

Gianna finally became so agitated about Miles that she sought to do something about it. The only thing she could think of doing was to go and see Ronnie Kray, who had by now set up his new empire in the Seven Sisters Road in north London. She knew what he was capable of from the Blind Beggar Pub killing in Whitechapel Road and from the rumours about the man Mitchell. Then at first hand she heard him say that McVitie wouldn't be around for much longer, and so it was. When she went in to see Ronnie, he was his usual charming self. Gianna explained that she had this problem with Miles, who was stalking her. She went on to explain that she had foolishly had an affair with him and that whilst she didn't want him hurt, she wanted him to be warned off in a way that would stop him from ever pestering her again. She was able to turn on the tears for Ronnie's benefit.

"Don't you cry, Gianna." Ronnie paused, thinking for a moment, and continued, "I could always have him castrated; that would put a stop to him forever, wouldn't it? I could get Reggie to do that for you. He's been talking about that method of dealing with people, as it happens."

The way in which Ronnie spoke made Gianna believe that he was totally serious about this. He was definitely not joking, and there was alarm in her voice when she reacted to this. "No, Ronnie, nothing quite as drastic as that please. I just want him frightened."

"Don't you worry, Gianna, I'll think of something. In fact, I know just the man."

"How much do you want me to pay you for this, Ronnie? I know these things must cost money, and I don't expect it for free. You must say."

"I don't want any money from you, Gianna. Consider it a favour that I am doing you—just keep encouraging all your lovely friends to keep coming to the club and playing the tables."

"Thank you so much, Ronnie. I don't want Carlo to know anything about this or he will cut me off without a penny."

"Stop worrying, Gianna, and consider it done. Just give me a week or so. If you are going to be at the Astor tonight, just point him out to me again so I know. I'll get his picture taken with me so that the boys have got a nice good, up-to-date mark on him."

This was Ronnie being very methodical. That evening, Ronnie and Reggie went to the Astor in Mayfair, and her usual friends were there, including Miles. Ronnie came over and made a big show of saying hello, winking at Gianna. He obviously remembered who Miles was without Gianna's assistance and singled him out, greeting him as if he was a long-lost friend. He signalled for a photographer to come over, and some shots were taken of their table, with Ronnie next to Miles with his arm around his shoulders. Gianna heard Miles say, "Trust Ronnie to get the evening going; isn't he a card?"

But as it turned out, it was to be the Krays' last night of freedom. After a long night of drinking into the early hours, they returned to their Finsbury apartment. At 5:00 AM, the door was knocked in and they were arrested. One can only wonder what would have happened to Miles if Gianna's request had been followed through. If he had fallen foul of the other London gang, the Richardsons, I expect he would have been nailed to the floor by Mad Frankie Fraser and had the odd toe removed by a bolt cutter. But by this time, they were already out of harm's way. I suppose that as it was, it would have probably been just a beating with a threat of worse to come if he didn't "lay off."

I don't think any event would have changed Gianna's fate, as by now it was the second week in May and Carlo had probably already hatched his plan. It could not have been at all pleasant for him to discover all the facts about her dissolute lifestyle, the men and women she slept with, or the fact that she thought he was useless in bed. These facts would have led to the elaborate plot to bring about her murder.

Carlo used his brother, who was devoted to him, to achieve this end. Gianna disliked brother Ronnie intensely and allowed it to show, and Carlo would have had no difficulty enlisting his support. He knew that Miles was sleeping with Gianna quite regularly, and the masterstroke was to involve him and later incriminate him. This was despite the fact that Ronnie carried out her murder late at night in the Mayfair apartment. Carlo must have hated her and not have been able to tolerate his humiliation any longer. He must have felt that he had given her everything during their married years together, and the sense of betrayal must have been more than he could stand.

For all of those years after the murder, Carlo kept up the pretence of keeping the family in Italy involved in his personal life, including his new family. This was much to the disgust of Hayley, who ended up marrying him. He even paid for my wedding to Dario, which in my mind made him into a god. Then there was the way he treated my two children as they were growing up. The generosity he showed toward them both was as if they were his own children. All of this put him way beyond suspicion.

He has cast a huge shadow over the lives of so many people, and as a result, so much ended in tragedy. I speak here for myself, my daughter, my son, his own sons Paul and David, who ended up marrying my daughter, and Hayley. This is not to mention the girl, Anna Castellani, who got involved in the plot in Venice when Paul was trying to uncover the killer of Gianna over thirty years later. This involved a staged incident in the Campo Santo Stefano that I am ashamed to say I played a part in, along with my then son-in-law David.

Also there was the impact on the life of John, Hayley's son by my father. He was good enough to return the diaries to me. He didn't have to do this, and I wonder whether he would have done so if he had been able to read German or had decided to get them translated. He was by now a wealthy man, inheriting most of the estate of his mother, who had been murdered by Carlo and Hayley's younger son, Paul.

Out of all the bad also comes some good, because it gave rise to other events. I wonder where I would be now be without Steve, who had gotten tangled up in the incident staged by Paul and David in the Campo Santo Stefano. I married him some time after his lovely wife Sam died quite suddenly. The events that took place in the Campo Santo Stefano also led to Robert, Steve's son, marrying Anna Castellani's best friend Francesca, who was also a part-time waitress at the café where the incident took place.

I managed somehow to hold my life together but acknowledge that I would never have been able to do this without my daughter, Maddalena. Sanity and perspective have been brought to my life by her and Steve, without whom I would never have attempted to tell this story.

CHAPTER 13

FINAL PAGES

Monday 4th August

Met Andrea in the Swiss Centre in Leicester Square for tea, and I was very interested to hear what it was she wanted to tell me as she had sounded quite mysterious over the phone. For ages she has been threatening to get a divorce from her husband Clive. Well now it is going to happen but not quite in the way that she was expecting. She wanted rid of him but was always worried about getting cut off without a penny if she left him. Apparently he came home from a business trip abroad, well not really, he had been away with someone else—and said that he had fallen in love with a younger woman and wanted to be free to marry again.

He told her that he was quite aware of what she had been getting up to and the part that I had played in the deceit by covering up for her. He was adamant that he wasn't going to change his mind no matter what she said. Does that mean that he knows about what I have been getting up to when I *haven't* been with Andrea? I hope not, so I pressed her—how much does he know, but Andrea couldn't tell me at the time, as it wasn't me she was thinking about.

Andrea says he wants an amicable divorce and she will get a lot less in the settlement if she chooses to fight it—he is determined to be fair, which must be a relief to Andrea. She seems to be quite relaxed about it all because she is getting what she wanted but I don't think she was too happy to learn that she was in her words being "traded in for a new model." She stands to be quite a wealthy woman in her own right and surprised me by then pleading with me to go travelling with her when it was all over and done with and she was finally free. I asked her for how long and she said for as long as possible—could I manage six months. That is a very long time and I said it might be too difficult but I think a month might be a possibility. I will tell Carlo when the opportunity arises nearer the time.

She asked me if things went well would I consider living with her and I said I would never be able to give that kind of promise and told her she was getting far too ahead of herself. She said I was right and apologised which she didn't have to do as far as I was concerned—it is quite obvious to me that she has been shocked by this, has thought about it, and just doesn't want to be lonely. I told her that she needs to give herself some more time to think things out. The truth is I don't think she really knows what she wants. She is worried about now being thirty years old. She also had quite a lot to drink.

I got home very late as a result which did not appear to please Carlo very much as he was already there when I arrived. He is going to Venice again and asked me if I wanted to go. I made my usual excuse despite the fact that he tried to tempt me with a stay at the Gritti. I told him that he should go with Hayley instead and teased him about her. She will love it—another chance to spend some time with my disgusting father who now makes a point of being home when he knows she is going to be there.

I feel bad about not seeing Luisa and must try and get her to come over here soon. Carlo says that her latest boyfriend is like a lap-dog and that she gives him a hard time—just like the hard time he says I give him. He is always saying that. At least there is going to be a party chez Miles on Wednesday. I think he is beginning to get the message that time between him and me is running out but I suppose I still like going around there. He is still very good to me but I am now bored with him and the sex with him is as ever extremely dull and predictable. I think he is going to take it very badly when I say it is over.

Tuesday 5th August

Carlo went to work in a bad mood. This is due to my reluctance to go to Venice with him. Perhaps I should make more effort. I will perhaps call in at the gallery tomorrow and surprise him and say I am taking him for lunch, that's if I can find out if he's going to be there. I am determined to make more of an effort in future and am going to make a start by getting rid of Miles. I really can't afford for Carlo to find out about him and it has gone on for too long.

It is unfortunate that my plan to warn him off couldn't be put into practice because I know it would have worked. I wonder what Ronnie Kray was arranging. I was thinking about Andrea and the phone went and who should it be but her—how often does that happen? She said sorry for going a bit far yesterday and hoped I would still be on for going out on Thursday night. Apparently Jo-Jo and Susie want to meet up in the Unicorn in Duke

Street and we can go on from there. I expect Andrea will want me to stay over though she didn't say. I hope she doesn't get badly drunk in reaction to what has happened. What she did say was that she asked Clive (her husband) what he meant about me and apparently all he knows is that Andrea and me are bisexual, something that really disgusts him apparently. He didn't say anything at all about Miles Wilson or Carlo so that is a relief.

I have written a letter of apology to Gerry and Gill. I haven't seen them since that night I played that trick upon them and it has been playing on my mind. Well they didn't have to stay all night. I just wonder if they are still together—somehow I doubt it. She will be off to University in a couple of months—perhaps he will be back in touch when she is no longer around. I would like to see him now and again.

I have started to think about what Carlo said a couple of months ago. Maybe I should go back to Venice and do some work for the Galleria. If I could get an apartment over there then I could alternate between there and London. I could invite friends over from London to stay with me and be away from Carlo's attentions. It would see the end of Miles and I could also be more in touch with Luisa without seeing my father. I will speak to Carlo about it and see whether he will fund the idea. I actually have the money to do it myself but don't want to break into it unless I really have to.

Wednesday 6th August

I surprised Carlo by dropping in and taking him to lunch. It was only to the Europa Sandwich Bar in Swallow Street but I like it there because the family running it are from Italy. They are always so nice in there. It was all going well until I mentioned my idea to him about living part of the time in London and part of the time in Venice. He was very lukewarm about it. I got upset at his reaction reminding him that he had recently said that my life lacked any focus and that I needed something to occupy my time and mind.

He said that he couldn't actually see that it would involve me doing very much other than pleasing myself. He put the onus upon me to contact the Galleria dell'Accademia in Venice to see if they had any positions and what role I could perform for them. I told him that I didn't expect him to contact them and I would do it. Even so he doubted that there would be anything for me but he would go along with it if he thought it was going to be something substantial and if it also increased the amount of work he could do for the Galleria back here in London. He went on to say that if I was to act as an agent then the expense of setting up there could be justified and the costs written off. It would have to be a full-time operation as far as he was concerned because it would mean further expanding contacts not just in Venice but in other major cities.

I didn't like the way he was turning this idea into something that just suited him. I reminded him it was not just about him and what he wanted but also what I wanted. I told him that I was not prepared to go running around all over Italy. I let my anger show a bit and in retaliation said that I would perhaps instead contact Luisa to see if I could do tour guiding like her. He said that was okay in summer but what about winter when all that kind of thing slackened off. He still said that there was a useful role I could perform at his gallery here in London. I had to once again tell him that I was not prepared to be in the same working environment as people like his brother and that disgusting man Brian Josephs so I am afraid that we did not part on the best of terms. The prospect of working with Hayley is not something I am prepared to consider and I told him so. It seems like I will have to break into my own money if this plan of mine is going to happen.

Things cheered up a bit when we went over to Miles' place for a cocktail party and it was as if we hadn't had words. Carlo will be off to Venice on behalf of the Tate Gallery where Miles works. He said to Miles quite pointedly that unfortunately I won't be coming with him and put that hard done by look on his face. I walked away at this point to talk with one of the serving girls. The firm of caterers Miles uses employs young and attractive serving girls and I have arranged to meet this one on Friday by which time Carlo will have gone to Venice with Hayley. Her name is Candy, which she tells me is short for Candice. She has blonde hair and unusually green eyes. The Champagne was certainly flowing well at the party and in order to avoid a big hangover I drank an equal amount of water during the evening. It meant lots of trips to the loo but seemed to work as I had no after effects—well nothing to speak of. Miles says he wants to speak with me and will phone on Thursday.

Thursday 7th August

Got up late this morning and started to write a letter to the Galleria in Venice but changed my mind. It will be better to go and see them in person. I will go with Carlo next time and see Luisa about guiding if the conversation with the Galleria is not a successful one. I think Carlo wants me in London where he can keep an eye on me. Perhaps it is time for me to change my ways—but not yet. Miles phoned and said that with Carlo away it would be a great idea to meet up and have dinner. I agreed to this but what he doesn't know is that I am going to finish with him for good. I don't need his money any more and I must stop seeing him.

I met the girls in the downstairs bar at the Unicorn as arranged. We had something to eat and I was surprised that it was quite good as pub food is not as good as people think it is. Andrea has obviously told the other two about her divorce and Susie said from now on she was going to have to be much more careful. She wants Harry to give her a large sum of money to go and get lost but I wonder how much that would take her outside of her comfort zone. This is what Andrea is finding out about now. Did I read that divorce was another form of widowhood?

We went on to the Astor and all reflected that it had somehow lost its edge since the Krays no longer went there. You don't get the same number of celebrities in there any more. I suppose it will change in time. I went back and stayed with Andrea who thankfully didn't get drunk as I feared she might. She is talking more sensibly now but still wants me to go travelling with her. I told her that it was a possibility but also had these plans about splitting my time between London and Venice. Her face actually brightened because she saw the opportunity to come and stay with me for a while if I got myself set up there. She even mentioned paying her way and helping to share the cost, which brings it another step nearer as far as I am concerned. As we lay in bed together I told her about all the places I would take her to see. I had been talking away for quite a long time before I realised that she had fallen asleep. I must be getting boring or perhaps the drink she consumed finally caught up with her and she just crashed out.

Friday 8th August

Carlo must have been up and away quite early this morning. I got back from Andrea's just after 7:00 AM and he had already gone leaving me a note. It was affectionate enough and it said he would call. There was half a chance that he may be back very late on Saturday or on Sunday morning particularly if things went well. Well I'm not waiting in for any calls and he can stay there for as long as he likes as far as I'm concerned. If he thinks that I am going to run around all over Italy for him then he is in for a rude shock. I was going to spend a day helping out at the gallery today because of the new exhibition but it turns out that in his absence Carlo has persuaded Miles to go over and keep an eye on things over the weekend. That means I don't have to do it.

This actually also suits Miles because he says he can easily slip out and have dinner with me at Stones Chop House in Panton Street. It's a bit stuffy and formal in there but I think I can endure it and will just see how the evening goes. I met Candy at the Café Royal and we drank Champagne cocktails in the bar before going on to Leicester Square for some disco dancing. We kept getting pestered by young men and when two of them became persistent we complained to the management who had them removed. Later on we went back to the Café Royal and much to my delight found Jo-Jo and Susie in there and we spent the rest of the evening with them before going back home. We all got a bit drunk and Susie started to play up to the barman, who despite her provocative behaviour remained cool and a model of restraint.

Candy, although two years younger than me, turned out to be an experienced girl in need of no encouragement so that was a pleasant surprise for me. She told me that the moment she saw me at the party she wanted to fuck me. It turns out that she is from southern Ireland and she is only working over here temporarily. We have arranged to meet again in late September when she is back from her holidays. I hope to have made some progress with my plans by then so it is a meeting that might not happen. She is one that I would like to see again—it is rare for me to have such an intense orgasm but she had the ability to make it happen twice once with her fingers and then with her tongue.

Saturday 9th August

This is a day that I will not forget in a hurry. Candy had no sooner gone at about 9:30 AM when Andrea turned up reminding me that we had agreed to go shopping and for lunch. I was only partly dressed which seemed to get her quite excited. She must have thought that it was for her benefit and I didn't like to tell her that I was still recovering from my night of passion with Candy. There was no point in hurting her feelings although I don't want her getting over-possessive like Hayley. Let's hope that doesn't happen. I shut the door of the bedroom and got dressed while she made coffee for us both.

This is when the entries finished; Gianna had started to write about the day when the sound at the door interrupted her. Gianna returned very late from her last meeting with Miles and the day's entry had just been started. It was that night that she was murdered by Ronnie, a plan that had been hatched by Carlo, who was away in Venice at the time. I wonder if she would ever have put those ideas she had to the test by escaping back to the city that she had fled from just four years previously. I got the impression from reading the diaries that she had a very low boredom threshold.

If, earlier on, she had decided to pursue a proper career, then it is likely that she would have not strayed as much as she did. Even right up to the time of her death, the last three nights had been spent with different lovers, one male and two females. That is the behaviour of a serial adulteress who was completely out of control. Carlo had already made up his mind that enough was enough. Even if she had not played into his hands and seen Miles that night, I think he would have found another way of getting rid of her.

I doubt if she had disappeared off to Venice as she was planning that it would have made any difference. A fatal "accident" would no doubt have befallen her sooner or later. If Carlo was alive today, the question others would ask him was why did he not just divorce her? The answer lies partly in these diaries. A divorce would have meant a financial settlement of some kind, and I don't think he wanted to get in a court battle that might reward her for the behaviour that he had put up with, but more than this, I think he was hell-bent on revenge for the humiliation he had suffered.

The diaries tell an unhappy tale and I don't really know what to do with them. Do I keep them for posterity or do I follow my husband's advice and burn them?

VENETIAN TRILOGY

Extract from Chapter 1 of book 1 in the trilogy, *Il Complotto* (The Plot)

CHAPTER 1

1968 – GIANNA

Charles Court, proprietor of the 'Gallery 107' on Jermyn Street, Piccadilly, put the telephone down on his conversation with Miles Wilson at the Tate Gallery. He did this with rather exaggerated care as his mind had already moved forward on to what he had to do next. These thoughts slowed down his movements. Miles Wilson had asked him to go out to the Galleria dell' Academia in Venice. He was to negotiate the loan of a selection of Venetian artists' pictures for the autumn exhibition at the Tate. His extensive knowledge of Venice and Venetian Renaissance art made him the obvious man to carry out the negotiations. Well, these were the words that Miles used. Charles and Miles didn't discuss the cost or fees involved – it was taken as read that Charles would be remunerated and reimbursed for all he did. Anyway they both came from social backgrounds where it was considered vulgar to discuss money. Miles's last words had been that he and Gianna, Charles's wife, should come over for cocktails; something that did not fill him with great enthusiasm as the way that Miles tended to dispense his largesse was always completely overdone. He agreed nonetheless, as this was to suit him with the arrangements he was going to have to make. His thoughts again turned toward Miles and his mind flitted from one aspect of his character to another. On a business basis he was easy to deal with and he now owed him a favour in return for the Venice trip. On a purely social basis part of the problem with him was that he was a great one for the ladies, and his behaviour was, at times, embarrassing and tiresome; even though most women found him harmless and amusing. When entertaining at home, Miles acted out the role of lounge lizard, perhaps because he enjoyed this alter ego. But Charles reflected that this was no alter ego. In reality, he *was* a lounge lizard. Still, enough of these thoughts! He had allowed his mind to wander so he reverted back to what he had been requested by Miles to do.

The important thing, as far as he was concerned, was that the Italians in Venice were very favourably disposed towards the British at the present time due to the help they received during and since the flood disaster not yet two years ago. This would count in his favour. The level of devastation in the city had been terrible with the water in Piazza San Marco reaching as high as six feet above the ground. The city was still recovering and it would be some time before things really returned to normal there. His wife's family over in Venice put on a brave face at the time of the disaster and was thankful that the apartment where they lived was not on the ground floor. It was a terrible experience to be without heat and light for a number of days. And of course there was the filthy water and the overpowering smell, enough to make anyone retch.

In basements, oil tanks burst adding to problems and it seemed there were dead pigeons to be found everywhere, floating on the surface and rotting. A nasty film of oil rested on top of the floodwaters. He wanted to see how things had improved since his last visit and how well the clean up and renovations were progressing. The work took a long time to get going because of all the surveys that had to be carried out. The International appeal for "Venice in Peril" had been set up and money came in from all sources to save the city and was still arriving. He had played an active part in raising money and it had not gone unnoticed in the Italian art world.

As a result, Charles had the impression from Miles that he would be pushing at an open door as far as the Italian gallery was concerned. All he had to do was get the right pictures. The only problem was that this request from the Tate came at a particularly busy time because of the current exhibition that he was trying to arrange at his own gallery on Jermyn Street. This trip was going to clash with his plans. But never mind, thinking about it logically, this could be turned to his advantage. In any case, he loved to go to Venice and this provided him with the excuse that he was looking for. He played things over in his mind for about half an hour while making notes on his office notepad, and then set about his planning.

He first telephoned Gianna and told her the dates that he was going to be away, giving her the exact timings. As usual, he asked her if she would like to come and take the opportunity to see her family. Not to his surprise, she said that she didn't want to go. Gianna never wanted to go to Venice these days. It was not just the recent flooding that made her a reluctant visitor. He decided to discuss this with her later. Secondly, he confirmed that Hayley, his personal assistant, was available for the days in question and gave her instructions to telephone the family in Venice to let them know he was coming and to book the flights with the British Airways Office on Lower Regent Street. Then finally he called up his elder brother Ronald on his internal telephone extension. Ronnie answered after the second ring. Charles summoned him to the office.

Charles took pity on his elder brother. He never had the benefit of a public school education like Charles. When Ronnie came into the world it was a difficult birth and he nearly died and he was left with certain disadvantages. He was a slow learner at school, and as a result was treated as a simpleton. His parents transferred him to a special school for young people with learning difficulties. When he was growing up, Charles often heard his parents talking about Ronnie being backward whilst other members of the family would cruelly refer to him as being mental. On leaving the special school, he had no qualifications. He then had a number of manual jobs, all of which had been unsuccessful until he was taken on by Westminster City Council as a garden labourer. This turned out to be satisfactory but he was not able to move in the same circles as his smart and handsome younger brother. As he grew older, he found his own level but the result was that he ended up mixed in with some fairly undesirable types. He had discovered that if you could make a big show of drinking, gambling and behaving in a riotous fashion that you would gain a certain notoriety and popularity with less intelligent people who were also inclined to act in the same way. This popularity was only superficial but Ronnie never really appreciated that fact. Amongst his so-called friends, Ronnie's large physical presence was useful whenever arguments would start and boil over into fights. Ronnie and his friends liked to go to football at Millwall Athletic Football Club and enjoyed the buzz of a good scrap with visiting fans. Ronnie and friends didn't invite trouble; they just went out and made trouble. That was when Ronnie would really come make his presence felt. He had little appreciation of the extent of his own strength and one night it got him into serious trouble. After a home match, in a typical Saturday night pub brawl at Southwark Bridge, Ronnie who had admittedly been severely provoked, knocked out another drunken imbecile and put him into a coma from which he never regained consciousness. Ronnie was arrested and charged. He spent some time on remand before the case went to court where he was convicted of manslaughter. He ended up being sent down and did a stretch in prison that was reduced to five years on account of his exemplary behaviour and of course, the influence of his brother Charles. Charles felt an enormous sense of guilt that he had prospered whilst his brother had been condemned to a poor life because of an accident at birth.

Charles had therefore been very supportive throughout this crisis and used his contacts to ensure that Ronnie got a sympathetic parole hearing when the time came. He visited him regularly in prison and was instrumental in getting him transferred to an open prison during his period of incarceration. The regime at this prison was a lot more relaxed and Ronnie became a popular and well-behaved inmate, a model prisoner. Charles made him promise to behave and do exactly as he was told. He promised Ronnie that he would get him out of prison quicker if he behaved. In the meantime, Charles promised the authorities that Ronnie would stay out of trouble by coming to work for him in the gallery. He would give him full-time work, training, and a home. When he was released, he duly came to work at the gallery. Ronnie occupied a small flat above the gallery and was, in effect, a resident caretaker. Ronnie really enjoyed this. In his eyes, it gave him a bit of status and it allowed him to live in the centre of town. One of Ronnie's pleasures was to wander around the pubs and clubs of the West End of London taking in the lights and visiting the various strip joints. He promised Charles that he would never go to football or associate with his old football-supporting friends again. He kept this promise. Whilst at work, Ronnie operated on a fairly simple level and Charles gave him jobs around the place involving all the manual duties including lifting, fetching, and carrying. He also paid for Ronnie to learn how to drive. Ronnie turned out to be a natural driver but failed the test three times before finally passing because he had difficulty mastering the Highway Code. Charles was patient enough to spend hours with him, helping him to learn it. Ronnie could be used very effectively as a blunt instrument with his menacing physical appearance but that was about it. He could also be a very effective minder, not only of Charles, but also of the paintings and objet d'art on display in the gallery exhibitions. Ronnie, for his part, worshiped Charles and basically did anything he asked of him.

Charles heard Ronnie knocking at the door and called out for him to come into the office. He settled him down before speaking to him in a low voice. He always made sure that he kept direct eye contact with Ronnie when speaking to him because this was the only way he could be sure that Ronnie was taking in what was being said. Ronnie usually had a very short attention span. Charles commenced what he had to say with deliberate slowness maintaining this lowered tone of voice.

"Ronnie, I'm going to Venice for a few days and there are some very important things that I want you to do for me while I'm away. Firstly, I am going to tell you why they need to be done. Secondly, it is very important for you to follow my instructions to the letter as it affects everybody in the business and therefore in the family as well. These things will need to be correctly carried out. Can I rely on you?"

Ronnie sat up and knew that he had to concentrate fiercely on what Charlie was saying. In an anxious tone, he replied in his south London accent, which was in complete contrast to the middle class refinement of his younger brother.

"Of course, Chas. You know that I would never let you down – you only 'ave to ask."

"All right Ronnie, you can relax. We are going to plan this together, right? It's a bit complicated."

"Yes, Chas."

"Good. It's going to involve you getting things ready for the next exhibition but other important matters as well. The consequences of you not following my instructions could be very serious so it is essential that you get things right. I don't mind how many times I have to go over it with you because it is so very important. All that we talk about is between you and me and nobody else. Is that clear?"

It was clear. This always made Ronnie feel that he was a key man. When Charles had given his extensive instructions, he finished his meeting with Ronnie. He made Ronnie go back over everything that had to be done until he was satisfied that he fully understood. Now that he set out the plans for what should be done whilst he was away and he turned his mind toward the business to be carried out in Venice. Ronnie left the room as he usually did when his brother had given him things to do – as if on a mission. Only this time it was going to be more complicated than before and very serious. After what he was told he had to do he now was experiencing a mild headache. No mistakes, Charlie said no mistakes. He must get things exactly right. The family and the business must not suffer. He knew that if he did get things wrong Charlie would be very annoyed and it could have disastrous consequences. Stick to the plan and everything would work out.

When Charles arrived home that evening at about half past five, he found once again that Gianna was out. Later on in the evening, at around eight o'clock, she returned, giving no explanation as to where she had been. Charles decided not to ask her. He found that it was better that way even though he was annoyed that he had to get his own dinner, especially after the day he had. When she was ready, she would talk about her day but she appeared to be in no hurry to do this. So instead, he engaged her in conversation about his upcoming trip. He described what he was going to have to do before turning to personal and family matters. He only managed to partly capture her attention in trying to make her fully aware of what he was saying.

"Of course I'm sad that you don't want to come to Venice. Naturally I will be going to see your family. What do you want me to say to them this time?"

"About what exactly?" Gianna replied, irritated he was asking.

"You know – the reason why you didn't want to come this time."

"Nothing. You are going on business and that is nothing to do with me. Tell them I will be over next time. I'm sure you will enjoy going over there. You always do. You don't need me to be there do you? You will enjoy seeing Luisa and father. Give Luisa my love."

"I will. She reminds me of a younger you." He paused and then continued, "I always say that, don't I? She has a new boyfriend I understand. His life will be hell. Like mine."

Gianna didn't even laugh at the joke. It was one that he had made several times before. Sensing that there was some tension building up, she then sought to justify her position. Years of living in London meant that it was difficult from her voice to know that she was from Italy; except for the fact of course that she still tended to use Italian for names and places.

"Well Carlo, you know that Venezia does not have the same fascination for me as it does for you. If you had been born and brought up there, then you might feel the way I do. To you it is like a drug going over there. For me, it is a drag not a drug and a reminder of a childhood that was restricted by the very isolation of the place from the rest of reality. There are too many tourists and too many mosquitoes in summer and the canals smell when it gets too hot. In the winter, it is bleak and cold with all of those horrible mists that roll in off the lagoon."

Charles held up his hand so as to prevent the excuses being trotted out.

"OK Gianna, you have made these points many times and I won't make you do what you don't want to do. It just does get difficult to explain though to the family. It is almost as if you don't want to see them anymore. Just think of what they had to go through that autumn and Christmas with those dreadful floods."

Gianna was ready for this and had her answer. "And you invited them here for Christmas – and they said no. They could have said yes – but they didn't."

"That's because they wouldn't leave their home, especially at a time of great stress and worry – and you know that. My God you are heartless at times!"

"No, it just underlines why I live here with you in London and not there. I don't want to walk through Piazza San Marco with my wellington boots on every time there is a high tide. The flooding over there is getting worse and worse. What happened there a couple of years ago is sure to happen again soon and I don't want to be there when it does."

Inwardly Charles wished he hadn't said what he did. He had allowed the irritation to enter into his voice. Her almost casual indifference towards her sister and father rankled. And if Venice was both crowded and bleak, what was London like in comparison? What she had said about the city was partly right. The "Venice in Peril" appeal had emphasised that unless something was done, then the city would one day be lost. But in her case, he felt it was just being said as a very convenient excuse.

"The other day you were saying that you wanted to return there, so which is it?" This did not get a response. He tried one more time. "Look, I can always get Hayley to change our reservations. We can always get an extra flight and instead of me going to stay with the family, we can book into to the Gritti Palace. You love it there."

"Not this time Carlo. You can enjoy the company of Hayley instead. I know how much she admires you. You need to watch her. I have seen the way she looks at you."

At least now she was smiling in the way she always did when she was teasing him. However, the fact was that Gianna preferred the company she kept here in London more than going back to her birthplace in the company of her husband. Her father now complained bitterly that she was English in her outlook and it was difficult to disagree with this. He even called her "my English daughter". Charles was not overly fond or even vaguely impressed with the people she associated with in London. Most of them behaved in a very pretentious manner and played up to Gianna. She either could not see this or simply enjoyed the flattery. Gianna enjoyed the clubs, restaurants, and casinos, especially when someone else was paying. She often complained that Charles kept her short of money, a fact that restricted the frivolous lifestyle that Charles believed she pursued. Getting a job was something that didn't occur to Gianna, not as she was married to a rich Englishman. Recently she had shown signs of wanting to be more financially independent but not in a way that he approved of. Even if Gianna had noticed the edge in his voice, she pretended that she had not. As Charles did not want to create a bad atmosphere, he mentioned that Miles had invited them for cocktails and that would give her a chance to meet up with some mutual friends. At least when this suggestion was made her mood seemed to lighten a little more but only momentarily. Gianna seemed to like Miles because he was always paying her very flowery compliments, and of course always served champagne to his guests. Gianna believed that Miles had a certain style but Charles didn't agree finding his behaviour somewhat louche.

It was two days after the cocktail party at the mews house in Pimlico where Miles lived that Charles telephoned Miles at the Tate. It was a successful evening. Gianna enjoyed being there and Miles enjoyed showing off in front of his guests as usual.

"Miles old man, it's Charles. Good party the other night. Gianna loved it – bit of a sore head the next day though."

"Charles, dear boy, you are most welcome. Tell me are you all set for Venice?"

"Yes! Listen Miles, I need a favour old man."

"Ask away, after all I do owe you one."

"Well as you know this Venice thing clashed with the preparation of this private showing I am doing at 107. I'm forced to rely on Ronnie putting everything together. He's in the showroom on Saturday and working overnight into Sunday as a matter of necessity. He's had his instructions, bless him, but sometimes he doesn't quite get things right. I was wondering with me being away whether you could drop in and see if he's OK? Use one of the flats over the office on the top floor if you like if it means staying over. Ronnie occupies the other one anyway but he won't disturb you. If it's too much of an imposition please say no, Miles.

"Well I think I can do that." I may have to pop in and out but so long as that is OK, I am sure that I can fit in with the scheme of things whilst you're away."

Actually it would fit in very well with the evening that Miles had planned but there was no need to go into detail telling Charles about that. And as for Ronnie, Miles found it was best to treat him like an old long lost friend. Charles had always told Ronnie to be very respectful to Miles and as ever Ronnie always obeyed his instructions.

Charles then replied, "Of course Miles. You come and go as you please. I expect that Ronnie will want to slip out at some stage as well. He likes to go down to Leicester Square for the odd pint or two but he's got his own key, so don't worry. You've still got yours to 107, haven't you?

"Yes I keep it here."

"Marvellous old chap! The main point is that someone needs to be there at all times otherwise the insurance will be invalid. I won't be back until Monday, no Tuesday, but I will get a message sent to you by telex to confirm that things have gone to plan or if there is any hitch."

"Fine. Goodbye Charles and good luck. Don't worry about the gallery. Give my best wishes to Venice. I wish I were going!"

"Thanks Miles, bye."

VENETIAN TRILOGY

Extract from Chapter 1 of book 2 in the trilogy,
Il Segreto (The Secret)

CHAPTER 1

2006

Maddalena Ongaro looked again at her name printed inside her passport. She had just woken up but it was still the early stage of her flight from Sydney to Rome. Emerging from a light sleep she momentarily had not been sure where she was. It was a long and frustrating delay before the passengers could embark on to the Alitalia flight but eventually they got under way. When settled in her seat it was not long before she had closed her eyes, almost as if she was trying to get the experience of queuing and waiting and queuing again out of her system. She had gone through this process so many times before yet still she hated this essential part of international travel, which at every stage was governed by the need for intense security. Now that she was fully alert she was carrying out the series of personal checks that many nervous travellers do to make sure they have got everything around them and on them. Everything was still there. It was now two weeks since she changed back to her maiden name; it was all part of her emotional catharsis. This followed the divorce from her husband. It had been the final trip that tied up all the loose ends. Now there was no turning back.

As far as she was concerned she was returning for good to her native Italy and this was something she never thought she would do until a couple of years ago. As the 747 Boeing cruised at 33,000 feet, first towards Singapore for a stop and then on to Rome she had time to reflect, firstly on her life before she emigrated about eleven years ago, then on the life she finally left behind in Australia and lastly to wonder what the future held for her.

At thirty-five it wasn't too late to start a new life and indeed she had already made strides in that direction. She remembered all those years ago when she was first married, she started her life in Sydney and was told by some friendly neighbours who invited them to a beach party at Bondi – "You're an Aussie now!" She quickly adapted to the way of life, language and culture and now spoke English with an easily recognisable Australian accent. Deep down she still felt like an Italian and her regular return visits to her birthplace in Venice meant that she never forgot her roots. But her outlook on life was not totally Italian anymore. She could be described as having an Anglo-Australian perspective on life and events as they arose. Now that she was returning for good would she revert back to being Italian in outlook? She didn't think so.

She did not necessarily think that her way of living was so different from anyone else but so many unusual, not to mention unpleasant things had happened in her life so far that it was at times hard to take it all in. She wondered if it showed in her face. Now she had fully dealt with the latest change and staying with her husband was never an option after what happened. The next meeting with her mother Luisa in Venice was going to be a very difficult one and probably an intense affair because not everything was yet out in the open. It was time for her to rationalise the situation before coming to some form of reconciliation with her mother. But there were some shocks still left in store for her mother after this last visit. She supposed that if you have a large number of setbacks in life after a time you become shockproof. In that respect her mother suffered even more than her but some of mother's worst problems were of her own making.

It was a matter of some amazement to herself that her mother wasn't really completely screwed up. She did not think that there was too much more to discover about what had gone on in the past. However she hoped if there was still more to come out that once revealed it didn't have the effect of damaging her irreparably. The first thing to deal with when she returned was a funeral, just what she didn't need. Somewhere in between there had to be this long talk with mother because the time had come to say what should have been said a long time ago.

Maddalena Ongaro – the name reflected back at her from the laminated page – how was *she* coping? When she told some of her friends back in Sydney that she was going back to Italy for ever and would not be returning this time, they asked if it was because of her divorce or her family. She explained that it was both and that there were many problems still to resolve. Within her immediate circle of friends most knew something of what she had been through in the last couple of years, much of which had been spent back in Italy. Strangely enough, these couple of years brought a certain amount of stability and happiness and that was what was driving her on.

She must have been asleep for longer than she thought because on the overhead screen the journey map showed that the plane was leaving Australian airspace. This event in its own way felt quite symbolic. Her thoughts again turned to family. She recalled one of her colleagues at work saying sympathetically that you could choose your friends but not your family. How true that was.

She realised that the noise that woke her up was the sound of the trolley bringing a meal for the semi-comatose passengers in economy class. Maddalena found it difficult to get excited about airline food but the consumption of it managed to kill half an hour of the flying time. The coffee that followed the meal was indescribably awful. It always was on aeroplanes – why didn't she learn? For that matter, why didn't it get any better? She winced as she saw the brown sludge emerge from the spout of the big pot and almost changed her mind but couldn't summon the courage to make a nuisance of herself.

It was important to eat as she now had an occipital headache. With her, this came about as a result of the build up of stress and tension and to have one this early during the flight was not a good sign. She reached inside her airline shoulder bag which had been stowed under the aircraft seat and pulled out the extra bottle of water she asked the stewardess for and took a drink. It helped to take away the dull metallic taste of the coffee which made her tongue feel like a piece of carpet in her mouth. Keeping well hydrated on long flights was the right thing to do and was something she had learned over the years. She hated taking any kind of pills or tablets but if this headache continued she would just have to give in. After half an hour it showed no sign of abating so she gave in and the water bottle was opened again to wash down the pain relief tablets.

Her minded drifted and shifted around all the issues. There was too much going on up there inside her head – this was the real cause of the headache. She closed her eyes and thankfully was asleep again.

About the Author

Jeremy Gent, one of four brothers, was born in South London where he spent most of his youth before moving first to Hampshire and then to Cornwall. He qualified as an accountant working in both public and private sectors before becoming a lecturer and then freelance as a tax consultant. He has travelled around Europe and speaks both Italian and German. He is married with one grown up son.